COVET
NEIGHBOR
A TUCKER SPRINGS NOVEL

L.A. WITT

RIPTIDE
PUBLISHING

Riptide Publishing
PO Box 6652
Hillsborough, NJ 08844
www.riptidepublishing.com

Covet Thy Neighbor (Tucker Springs, #4)

Cover Art by L.C. Chase, lcchase.com/design.htm
Editor: Sarah Frantz
Layout: L.C. Chase, lcchase.com/design.htm

ISBN: 978-1-62649-001-7

First edition
March, 2013

Also available in ebook:
ISBN: 978-1-62649-000-0

COVET THY NEIGHBOR

A TUCKER SPRINGS NOVEL

L.A. WITT

To Sarah Frantz
For being even more terrifying as an editor than you were
as a reviewer. I love you for it! —L.A.

TABLE OF CONTENTS

Rain rolled off the awning above the front window of Ink Springs. On shitty days like these, Lane and I didn't even bother putting on the stereo. By the time we turned it up enough to hear it over the weather, it'd be too goddamned loud. So, the soundtrack for the day was thunder, rain, and buzzing tattoo needles, with occasional bits of conversation to fill in the gaps.

Not much buzzing today, though. As a rule, people didn't casually wander in here during storms, and half of this afternoon's appointments had called and canceled. Half the other ones probably wouldn't show up. Which meant two of my favorite things in the whole world: a slow, boring day, and not a lot of money. Fucking yay.

I scrubbed my workstation with a wadded, disinfectant-soaked paper towel while Lane sketched, pencil scratching across paper. Good thing he didn't mind chatting while he was drawing, because he'd probably be all the company I had today.

Lane got up from his chair to stretch, and glanced at the window. "Oh, man. I would not want to be moving on a day like this."

I looked up from cleaning. "Moving?"

He gestured out the window. Someone was backing a U-Haul into one of the parking spaces in front of the store.

"Aw, damn." I tossed the paper towel in the wastebasket and stood. "I forgot Robyn was moving out today."

"She is? Where the hell's she going?"

"Her girlfriend's got a house on the other side of town. They're shackin' up." I put on my jacket and started toward the door. "Since we're dead right now, I'm going to go see if she needs any help."

"Have fun. Don't get wet."

"Yeah, right." I stepped outside. Right next to the storefront was the doorway to the stairs leading up to my apartment. Up until today, the apartment across the hall from mine had been Robyn's. As she got out of the U-Haul, landing with a splash in a small puddle, I shouted over the rain, "You're really moving out? On a day like this?"

"What can I do?" Robyn held her jacket over her head and trotted up to the sidewalk and out of the rain. She lowered her jacket and shook off some of the water. "My lease is up tomorrow, and I can't change the weather."

"You sure it's not a sign from God, telling you to stay here?"

Robyn threw her head back and laughed. "Yeah, right. I believe that about as much as you do." She gave me a playfully condescending look. "Now, Seth. We've been over this, sweetheart. I still love you, but Krissy and I are moving in together."

I stomped dramatically on the wet pavement. "Fine. *Fine.* Just abandon me to whatever miscreants move into your apartment."

She patted my arm. "They'll fit right in around here, won't they?"

"Hey!"

She giggled. "Am I wrong?"

"Bitch."

"Whatever." Robyn elbowed me hard. "You're such a brat."

I laughed. "Anyway, you need any help?"

She shook her head. "There isn't much left. We're just down to the big stuff I couldn't fit into my car. Krissy's on her way, and she and I can handle that."

"You don't need a big strong man to carry the heavy stuff?"

"If I needed a big strong man, I'd come ask you who I should call."

"Ooh. Ooh. Robyn, I bleed."

She snickered. Then she plucked a white cat hair off my collar and flicked it away into the wind. "I am going to miss visiting Stanley, though."

"Well, you can always come see him," I said. "Door's always open for Stanley's buddies."

"You can't bring him over for a playdate with Jack and Sunny?"

"Um, no." I held up my hand and pointed at a couple of scratches. "Cats and car trips? Don't mix? Remember?"

"Oh, yeah." She smothered a laugh. "Big tough man getting his butt kicked by a fluffy kitty. That's so adorable."

I scratched my jaw with my middle finger.

"Such a gentleman. Anyway, I— Oh! I forgot to mention. Al called last night, and I think someone's coming to look at the place later this afternoon."

"Already?" I put a hand over my heart. "Well, I promise you I won't move on quite as quickly as Al has. I'll take some time to properly grieve and all that."

"Aww, you're such a sweetheart."

"I'll make sure to stand outside your new front door and serenade you with Justin Bieber tunes while—"

"Krissy has a twelve-gauge."

"Never mind."

Robyn laughed. "Okay, I should get to work before Krissy gets here and drags me upstairs by the ear."

"I'd pay to see—"

"Fuck you." She nodded toward my shop. "Get back to work, you slacker."

"All right, all right. But drop by the shop once in a while, will you? Let me know you're still alive?"

"I will." She hugged me tight. "Take care of yourself, sweetie."

"You too."

Robyn went upstairs to finish moving her things out of the soon-to-be vacant apartment, and I went back into my shop feeling just a little bummed out. Neighbors came and neighbors went, but after a string of really obnoxious ones, Robyn had been a refreshing change. We'd been good friends since about a week after she moved in.

We'd stay in touch, of course—it wasn't like Robyn was leaving the country or anything. It was her replacement who worried me. Much as I didn't believe in karma or any of that superstitious bullshit, it wouldn't have surprised me if the price for having a cool neighbor for the past three years was living across from a fucking psycho for the next three.

We shall see.

The U-Haul left, and the afternoon went on, getting progressively grayer and nastier by the hour. Fortunately, some bored and adventurous college students came in for ankle tattoos, which meant we had both cash flow and something to do. By five, I'd almost forgotten about impending Neighborgeddon, and was lost in inking a flowery design across a whimpering blonde girl's foot.

"Breathe, hon. The worst is almost over, I promise." I pressed the needle as carefully as I could over the bony spot I was working on. "It's always worst right on the bone."

"Oh, God . . ." She groaned.

I lifted the needle off her skin. "You all right?"

She nodded. "Just didn't think it would hurt this much."

Behind me, the front door opened, and I caught the last part of my landlord's sentence: ". . . can meet Seth. He lives in the apartment across the hall from the one you're interested in, and he owns this shop."

Over my shoulder, I said, "Be right with you, Al."

"Take your time, son."

I took my foot off the pedal and, as the needle's buzzing subsided, looked at the mirror above my workstation. This gave me a discreet vantage point from which to catch a glimpse of my potential new neigh—

Oh, *fuck*.

I'd joked with my buddy Michael for the last couple of weeks about all the different kinds of nightmarish neighbors who might take Robyn's place. Drunks who'd come home from benders and puke on the shared stairs. Horndogs who didn't realize how thin the walls were. Moochers. Serial killers. Drummers with insomnia.

But what had I not considered? The worst possible kind of neighbor.

Smoking hot eye candy.

With a goddamned boyfriend.

I didn't know which one was the neighbor, which one was the boyfriend, or if they were both moving in. Didn't matter, because they were both fucking *hot*.

Especially the slightly shorter one. They were both ridiculously fuckable. Like, "Don't even bother buying me a drink, I don't care what your name is, just drop trou and let's go" fuckable. But that second one, the one who was currently craning his neck to check out some of the art along the top of the wall, needed to spend some serious time bent over my bed. Even from here, his smile alone was enough that all that breathing and blood-flow bullshit was suddenly not happening the way it was supposed to. Intense, dark eyes. A short, perfectly trimmed beard framing his lips. Sharp cheekbones and jaw. If he had half a brain and a sense of humor, I was a dead man.

A cute twink with a devilish grin could turn me into putty, but this kind of guy? The fit, laid-back type who was effortlessly sexy even in a parka and with wind-messed, rain-dampened hair? Kryptonite-tipped arrow in my goddamned Achilles heel. *Fuck.*

I turned to my client. "Would you excuse me for just a second?"

She exhaled. "I could use a break for a few minutes anyway."

I smiled. "It won't take long, I promise."

While she rested her head against the chair and took some slow, deep breaths, I set the gun aside and peeled off my gloves. Then I headed toward the front of my shop to say hello to my landlord and the hotness that I hoped was moving in next door. Maybe I couldn't touch, but I could sure as hell take in the eye candy.

"Ah, here he is," Al said.

As the three men faced me, I extended my hand and even managed to choke out my name. "Seth Wheeler."

The shorter one looked me right in the goddamned eye as he shook my hand. "Darren Romero." Then he let me go and added, "This is my brother, Chris."

Brother? *Well.* That changed everything, didn't it?

As I shook hands with Chris, Darren gestured around the shop. "So you're an artist."

Chris didn't make a sound, but as he let go of my hand, a flicker of distaste crossed his expression. A slight curl to his lips, one eyebrow lifting in the slightest, briefest arch. Oh well. Fuck him.

I shrugged. "Artist. Skin defiler." I glanced at the girl who was still breathing deeply at my workstation. "College student mutilator. Really depends on who you ask."

Darren laughed when Chris rolled his eyes. "Oh, relax."

Chris glared at him. "You really think living in this part of town, on top of a tattoo shop, is such a good idea?"

The humor instantly vacated Darren's expression, and he said through his teeth, "We'll discuss this later."

The whole shop was suddenly tense. Even the girls who'd started chatting while Lane worked on one of their tattoos fell quiet.

"Anyway." Darren turned to me again and smiled, and the tension broke.

The girls resumed chattering. The tattoo needle buzzed back to life. Chris scowled and found something other than me or his brother to focus on.

I muffled a cough. "Uh, before I forget, there's a move-in discount." I nodded toward the artwork on the wall. "First tattoo is on the house."

Darren grimaced. "Oh. No. I don't do needles."

"Or tattoos," Chris grumbled.

Darren eyed him. "The needle kinda negates that part."

Chris started to say something more, but a pointed look from his brother shut him up.

"Well, damn." I sighed. "That's usually how I get to know my new neighbors."

"Is it, now?" Darren asked.

"It gets them in a chair for a conversation, anyway," I said. "Assuming they can handle the pain."

Darren shuddered. "I'll pass, but thanks for the offer. We'll just have to find another way to get to know each other."

The boldness of the statement startled me. Probably because I immediately read way too much into it.

I met his eyes, and he grinned, and it was one of those little *yeah, I'm flirting right back* grins. Read way too much into it, my ass. One eyebrow rose so slightly I was probably the only one in the shop who noticed, but it was more than enough to fuck up my balance. And he was going to be living across the hall from me? Right then and there, I gave it a week before he smiled at me or something and I ended up tripping over my own feet and going down the stairs on my ass.

And we were still staring at each other.

I broke eye contact and cleared my throat. "So are you new to the area? Like, just new to this part of Tucker Springs? Just moved here from another planet?"

Darren shifted his weight and glanced at Chris, but then smiled again—and damn, it seemed forced this time—as he said, "I just moved here from Tulsa." He gestured at his brother. "He's been here a few years and suggested it, so here I am."

"Yeah, but I wasn't expecting you to move into *this* part of town. Especially . . ." Chris scowled, giving the shop a sweeping look of obvious disapproval. "Are you sure you want to live on top of a place like this?"

"Don't worry," I said with a dismissive wave. "The Light District is totally quiet and safe. And as for living above a tattoo shop? All that nonsense you've heard about ink fumes bringing gremlins to life and causing buildings to teleport into parallel dimensions? Nothing more than unproven pseudoscience."

Darren laughed, but his less-than-amused brother said, "I'm more concerned about the people who hang around tattoo shops."

"Chris." Darren glared at him. To me, he said, "Sorry. I'm really not concerned about—"

"It's a tattoo shop in a college town," Chris growled. "With bars and clubs within vomiting distance." He pointed out at the street. "That sleazy club I told you about? Lights Out? It's right up the road."

"Actually, it's that way." I nodded in the other direction. "And it's not that sleazy."

Chris grumbled something I didn't understand. Then, to Darren, "How do you know this neighborhood's not going to be crawling with drunks and loud people at all hours of the night?"

I gritted my teeth. "Just don't bring your friends by, and we won't have to worry about any unsavory riffraff."

Al glared at me. So did Chris.

Darren just laughed. "I think the neighborhood's fine. Really."

His brother scowled again, but shrugged. "Well, you're the one who has to live here, not me."

Darren rolled his eyes. "If it gets unbearable, I'll come stay with you and Mona. Anyway, the neighborhood seems pretty nice. Might be better if management did something about"—he gestured outside—"the precipitation problem, but I suppose I can deal with it."

Oh, for fuck's sake. A dry sense of humor. I'm a dead man.

Al laughed and clapped Darren's shoulder. "I'll put in a request and see what I can work out." To me, Al said, "Assuming his credit and background checks go through and he doesn't change his mind, he wants to move in on Thursday. Would you and Lane mind parking behind the building that day?"

"Sure, no problem." I turned to Darren. "If you need a hand with anything, let me know. Thursdays are pretty quiet around here."

He smiled, which threw my pulse out of whack again. "Thanks. I should have it under control, but I'll keep it in mind."

Al herded Darren and Chris out of the shop, and I'd be damned if Darren didn't throw me one last glance—and one last *holy fuck* smile—before they continued out of sight.

I needed to get back to my client and finish her tattoo, but for a moment, I just stared at the empty doorway.

So Darren Romero was my new neighbor.

Hot. Potentially single. Potentially gay.

Maybe Robyn moving out wasn't so bad after all.

CHAPTER 2

As predicted, Darren moved in on Thursday. At least it stopped raining shortly before noon. Otherwise Chris would have had one more reason to glower and grumble when I came out to see if they needed a hand. Good thing Darren was the one moving in. Chris and I might've come to blows before the first day was out. Or he and a piece of furniture might have taken an *unfortunate* tumble down the stairs. This neighborhood didn't need another negative jackass. That was my job, damn it.

Chris's brother, however, was welcome to stay as long as he wanted.

Fortunately, I had plenty to distract me while that gorgeous piece of temptation moved in upstairs. Unlike most Thursdays, today was one appointment after another, all the way up until seven o'clock.

As the door banged shut behind my last client for the day, I closed my appointment book. Another day down, and a pretty damn productive one.

Lane had already gone home, so I cleaned up my workstation, locked up the shop, and headed outside for the horribly strenuous thirty-foot commute to my apartment.

I was reaching for the door to the stairwell when it opened. And just like that, I was face-to-face with Darren. He didn't look much different from earlier, though his damp hair was casually arranged, so he must've just had a shower. Still, his presence struck me like it had the first time, and there went my heartbeat and brain waves.

"Oh." He stopped. "Didn't realize you were off work already."

"Already?" I checked my watch, pretending my pulse hadn't just jumped. "It's quarter to eight."

"Aren't tattoo shops usually open late?"

"Yeah, on the weekends. Thursdays are . . . eh."

"Gotcha. So, um." He tucked his hands in his pockets and rolled his shoulders. "I'm still learning my way around this place. Anywhere you can recommend for a beer?"

How about my place? "All kinds of restaurants down that way." I gestured past him, toward the Light District's Town Square. "Just depends on what kind of atmosphere you're into."

"Something quiet is good," he said.

"I'd try Jack's. Just opened recently, and it's not one of those loud sports bar types."

"I think I'll give that one a try, then. Thanks."

"Don't mention it."

He started to go, but paused. "Do you, um, want to join me?"

I coughed to keep from choking on my own breath. "I—really?"

Darren shrugged. "Hey, I'm new in town. I'm all for any opportunity not to eat alone."

"So you're just using me for company until you make friends." I sighed and shook my head. "I'm touched, Darren. I really am."

He laughed. "Have to start somewhere."

"True, I guess you do." I put my keys in my pocket. "Sure. Let's go."

We started down the sidewalk. The only evidence of this morning's torrential downpour was the odd puddle, and the evening was cool but hardly unpleasant. Not a bad night for a stroll with the newest hot guy in Tucker Springs. As long as I managed to keep my feet under me, I was golden.

"So this seems like a nice neighborhood so far," he said after a while.

"Your brother didn't seem to think so."

Darren laughed softly, if a little halfheartedly. "He's just protective. You know how older brothers are."

The comment smacked me in the chest, but I didn't let it show. He couldn't have known.

I forced a smile. "Yeah, I know how they are."

"Sorry if he was a bit, um, abrasive the other day. And today."

"Don't worry about it." I sidestepped a small puddle. "But tell him you can pass the move-in discount on to him if he wants some free ink."

"Really?"

"Sure." I paused. "Can't promise I won't take a few liberties with his design of choice, but . . ."

Darren laughed with a little more enthusiasm this time.

Toward the end of the block, we slowed down beside the rainbow-festooned Pride shop. Flags, banners, posters, books; the place had it all. Darren scanned the colorful merchandise in the window as we walked past.

"They have places like that in Tulsa?" I asked.

"Not in my neighborhood," he said with what I thought was a hint of bitterness.

"You, um, you do know this is the gay part of Tucker Springs, right?"

"I do." He looked at me as we kept walking. "That's why I moved here."

"Oh. All right." So he *was* gay. Detail confirmed, target acquired. "Carry on, then."

"So what do you do around Tucker Springs?" he asked. "When you're not tattooing people?"

"Well, a buddy of mine and I know the biking trails by heart. You into mountain biking?"

"Mountains?" He threw me a sidelong glance. "I'm from Oklahoma. I get a bloody nose stepping onto a curb."

I laughed, not sure if it was his sense of humor or just those *eyes* that made my heart go crazy again. "The second-floor apartment must be hell, then."

"It's an adjustment, let me tell you. It'll be easier once my oxygen tanks get here, though."

Goddamn, he was quick. I liked.

I cleared my throat. "Okay, things to do in Tucker Springs that won't give you altitude sickness. There are some pretty good clubs around, especially here in the Light District. Buddy of mine owns Lights Out." I gestured over my shoulder in the general direction of Jason's club.

"Isn't that the one Chris was talking about? The sleazy one?"

I waved a hand. "What would a straight guy know about a gay night club?"

"Oh, yeah. Good point. So it's . . . a good one?"

"Probably the best on the singles scene."

"Good to know. Though clubs aren't generally my scene," he said. "Too loud, too . . . just not my scene."

"Understandable." But he hadn't mentioned that he was spoken for.

Jack's wasn't crowded, and the hostess quickly seated us by a window in the lounge area. We both ordered the local microbrew on tap, and then browsed the small menu in search of something edible.

I'd been grazing all day long, though, and Darren wasn't particularly hungry, so we settled on drinks.

"So, how long have you been in Tucker Springs?" he asked.

"Since college. About twelve years, now, I guess."

"What'd you study? Art major?"

"No, I was actually majoring in music theory. Planned to teach, but . . . I never finished. Dropped out my junior year." I took a long drink, as if that could begin to rinse the bitterness out of my mouth. "What about you? What brings you to Tucker Springs?"

"Work."

The single word gave me pause. Maybe I was imagining it, but something about his tone reminded me of the bitterness I'd just tried to wash off my own tongue.

Before I could ask, Darren cleared his throat. "I'd been in the plains too long, anyway, and needed a change of scenery. Thought the mountains would be a nice switch."

"Is it?"

He smiled. "So far, so good."

"Good. I think you'll like it here." *And you certainly won't hear me complain about you* being *here*. I took a quick drink. "Even if you don't like it right away, though, the place does grow on you after a while."

"I'll keep that in mind if I start questioning my decision to come here." He slowly swirled his glass, watching the remaining beer slosh inside. "So, the hiking is decent out here? Once I get used to the elevation, I mean?"

"The hiking is amazing. And some of the trails are fairly tame for wimpy lowlanders like you."

Darren threw me a playful glare. "Well, I wouldn't want to wind up on top of a hill and not be able to get back down, would I?"

I smirked. "Yeah, well, Search and Rescue only comes out if you're above three thousand feet. Anything lower than that, you're on your own."

He nodded sagely. "I'll keep that in mind. Maybe if I go exploring out there, I should take you along as a guide."

Oh, yes. Please do. "I'm always happy to show a newbie around the trails. You ever want to go, just give me a holler."

"I'll do that." He smiled, then sipped his beer. "So you mentioned the singles scene earlier. How is it in this town?"

I shrugged. "Not as big as it would be in Denver or someplace like that, but there's plenty of single guys on the prowl around here."

"You one of those guys?"

My throat tightened. "Are you asking if I'm single?"

He put his mostly empty glass down and looked me in the eye. "In a roundabout way, yes."

"I am." I reached for my beer. "And you?"

"For far too long, yes."

"Is that right?"

He nodded. "Kind of took a break there for a while. Had some—" His expression darkened briefly, his eyes losing focus. Then he shook himself back to life. "You know how it is. Life gets in the way, and the next thing you know, it's been forever since you've been out with someone."

I nodded. "Oh, yeah. I know how that goes." I raised my glass in a mock toast. "My last boyfriend and I split, God . . ." I paused, adding up the dates in my head. "Shit, it's been almost four years now."

"Wow, really?" Darren shook his head. "Hasn't been that long for me. I've only been out of the game for two."

"Well, I didn't say I'd been out of the game for four years." I grinned at him over the top of my glass. "Just said it's been four years since I've had a boyfriend."

"Ah, I see." He returned the grin, and then drained his glass. "You want another?"

"I could go for one more." I started to stand, but Darren put up a hand.

"This one's on me," he said.

"You sure?"

He nodded and got up. "Same thing?" He gestured at my glass. "The pale ale?"

"Yeah, that'd be great. Thanks."

He smiled. "Be right back."

I watched him go, and holy perfect body, Batman. His jeans weren't quite painted on, but they didn't leave much to the imagination. If they looked that good from this angle, then I needed to find something to hold my attention when he came back, or I'd be indulging my curiosity about how well they fit in the front.

Seth. Dude. What the fuck?

I shook my head and shifted my gaze out the window. It was too dark to see the mountains, but oh well. I focused on them anyway. Totally didn't watch Darren's reflection or anything. At all. Not even once. Especially not when he leaned over the bar. Or cocked his hip just a little.

Dude.

I rubbed my eyes. Okay, so he'd thrown me off-balance when he'd come into my tattoo shop the other day, and even now just watching him made me dizzy, but he was too perfect. There had to be something wrong with him, and now I caught myself waiting for the other shoe to drop. That one quirk, that one trait or something, that landed him very firmly in the friend zone. Or even the neighbor zone. Something heinous enough to disqualify him from my not-terribly-exclusive "fuck once and call it a day" zone.

So far? No dice. This guy checked all the boxes. Hot as all fuck. Dry sense of humor. Intelligent. Direct. Presumably employed, if his job had moved him out here. I didn't believe in bullshit like love at first sight, but the dial in my head had conspicuously turned from *I'd fuck you* to *I could see myself dating you. Which would include fucking, so it's all good.*

You've known him for an hour, idiot.

That other shoe could still drop. There was still time. It had taken my ex a solid year to reveal his rampant douchebaggery, so there was most certainly still time for Darren to prove he was way too good to be true.

"One pale ale," he said, drawing me out of my thoughts and back into his presence. He put the glass on the table before he sat across from me and wrapped his hand around his own drink.

"So, you mentioned before that work brought you out here," I said, trying to tread lightly and gauge his reactions since this didn't seem to be his favorite topic. "What is it that you do?"

Darren took a long swallow of beer. Then he set his glass down. "I'm a minister."

Record scratch.

"Sorry, what?"

He laughed. "A minister." He gestured outside. "Just started working for the New Light Church down the street."

"Oh." I took a drink. A *long* one. "Well, um, in the interest of full disclosure, I'm an . . ."

"Atheist?"

I blinked. "How did you know?"

Darren smiled. "God told me."

"Oh yeah?" I smirked. "What else did he tell you about me?"

"Well, that you'd be interesting enough to be good company for a couple of beers." He raised his glass. "I'd say He was right."

I eyed him. "Okay, seriously. How did you know?"

He threw his head back and laughed. "The 'Professional Skeptic' sticker on your truck kind of gave it away."

"Oh. Yeah. I suppose it would, wouldn't it?" I gnawed the inside of my lip. "So you already knew about that before you asked me to come out here tonight."

"No." He shook his head. "While the bartender was getting our beers, I ran back to where you were parked and checked your bumper for incriminating stickers."

"Smartass," I muttered into my beer. I rolled a sip around on my tongue for a moment, then swallowed it. "Funny. Most people in your . . . profession aren't too keen on having beers with guys like me."

He traced the rim of his glass with his middle finger. "Well, you might find that I'm not like a lot of people in my profession."

Yeah. We'll see about that. I tried to push back the bitterness that a cross or a fish inevitably raised, but it was a challenge. Damn it, I liked Darren, but his goddamned job made him off-limits for dating. Or anything else, for that matter.

Disappointing, but such was life. He was free to believe, just as I was free to not believe. It just put us very firmly off each other's menus. I had no doubt I was as far off his as he was off mine; how much had I heard in my religious days about the perils of being the only Christian in a relationship? About being unequally yoked? Yeah, this wasn't going to happen.

"So." I forced a grin. "Is this the part where we start loudly debating creationism versus evolution until they throw us out?"

He laughed. "We'd need a few more beers for that, don't you think? Maybe some tequila shots?"

"Good point."

Darren drummed his fingers on the side of his glass. "For what it's worth, I'm not usually the type to get into loud debates. I mean, not unless someone really wants to, but even then . . ."

"So I'd have to provoke you."

Laughing again, he shook his head. "You'd have to work pretty hard to provoke me into something like that."

I raised an eyebrow. "Then you, sir, are obviously new to the neighborhood, because that has 'challenge' written all over it."

Darren raised his glass. "Your funeral."

Fuck, dude. You are so *my type, you asshole.*

He took a drink, and as he put his glass down again, he said, "Also for what it's worth, we probably agree on more things than not. I'm sure I don't have to tell you that science and religion aren't mutually exclusive."

"Fair enough." I considered seeing what it would take to get him into a loud debate, but I was enjoying his company and my beer. "Well, beliefs aside, something tells me you and I are going to get along pretty well."

"I'm getting that distinct impression myself."

We let the topic of religion die, and bantered about safer subjects instead. All the while, as we drank and talked, I couldn't help feeling a little bummed out. After all, Darren had checked all the boxes and pushed all my buttons. Maybe I'd mistaken his lingering eye contact as flirty when it was just a sign of confidence. Maybe it was just wishful thinking that had made me drawing flirtatious, loaded conclusions from every move he made. Except, with the way he smiled now and then, or narrowed his eyes just right, it was hard not to read something into it.

But even if we were both flirting, the fact was that ministers didn't do one-night stands, and Seth Wheeler did *not* date Christians, never mind ministers. No matter how hot they were. Or how available. Or suggestive. Son of a bitch.

After we'd each finished a third beer, we left Jack's and wandered back toward our apartments. I opened the door beside my tattoo shop and gestured for him to go ahead. Good thing these stairs were dark: I couldn't see his ass, which gave me a reasonably good chance of making it to the second floor without breaking my neck.

The hallway between our apartments, however, wasn't so dark, and it wasn't Darren's ass that held my attention. Or mine that held his.

"Um." He shifted his weight, but still didn't break eye contact. "Thanks for . . . for showing me around the neighborhood."

"Yeah." I swallowed. "Don't mention it."

We shook hands, mostly because nothing else seemed appropriate at that moment, at least not to me, but still didn't walk away from each other. And didn't let go of each other's hands.

Eye contact. Broken. Eye contact. Broken.

God, he was gorgeous.

Seth. Dude. This way lies madness. Walk away. Walk the fuck away.

Darren chewed his lip and met my eyes. "So, this might be a bit forward, but I'd like to see you again."

"You will." I grinned in spite of the way my heart had just accelerated and the fact that I hadn't yet let go of his hand. "We live in the same building."

Darren laughed. "You know what I mean."

"Yeah, I do, and I—"

He used his grasp on my hand to pull us together, and kissed me. The motherfucker *kissed* me.

Not fair. Not fair at all. It was a crime against humanity that a man this hot and this amazingly aggressive was also one of—*fuck*, I didn't care. I just wanted him. I cradled the back of his neck and parted my lips for his insistent tongue. Jesus, he cut right to the chase. Straight for the deep kiss from the get-go, and two could play at this game.

I pulled him closer, kissed him harder, and he growled softly, digging his fingers into my shoulders.

He broke the kiss as abruptly as he'd started it, and held my gaze. "Wow. I . . ." He swept his tongue across his lips. "I wasn't quite expecting . . ."

"That makes two of us."

He blinked. "I . . . I'm sorry. I'm not usually this . . ."

"I didn't say it was an unpleasant surprise."

"Well, no, okay, it—" He took a breath. "I'm not normally so . . ."

"Aggressive?"

"Yeah. That. Not with someone I just met."

"Well, if it's any consolation—" I shoved him up against the wall. "—I am."

He shivered, and I had a split second to remember he was *a damned minister* before we were kissing again, and from his kiss, I wondered if maybe he'd forgotten too. Or just didn't care. Whatever. I kissed him harder, pressing into him and groaning when he pressed back.

Once again, we broke away, and once again, we stared at each other. My hand was on his neck. Both of his were on my waist, tugging just slightly at my belt loops like he didn't want me to pull back. The tension thrumming between us was impossible to read. Disbelief? Pure arousal? I didn't know anymore. I knew I was hard, I knew I wanted him, and I knew there were reasons I shouldn't even let myself fantasize about this going any further.

Guys like him don't do things like this with guys like me.

Guys like him don't do *this.*

Darren's eyes darted toward his door. "You want to come inside? For . . . a drink?"

My heart sped up. "You actually feel like a drink right now?"

Darren held my gaze. Then he tightened his grasp on my belt loops. "Not really, no."

"Then what . . ." I hesitated. "What do you feel like right now?"

"What do you think?"

I think I want you. I think you want me. I think . . . I think . . .

He spoke first: "Question."

I lifted my eyebrows, but didn't say anything.

One corner of his mouth rose, and his eyes narrowed just right to fuck with my blood pressure all over again. "Door number one?" He nodded toward his apartment, then mine. "Or door number two?"

All the air in the hallway disappeared.

"Are you—" I cleared my throat just to get some air moving. "Are you serious?"

"You'd better believe it."

And he kissed me again.

CHAPTER 3

T hat kiss ended in a rush of breath from both of us.

I touched my forehead to his. "Holy fuck." My tight grip on the back of his neck was the only thing that kept my hand from shaking. "And here I thought you just wanted to get beers."

"I did." He brushed his lips against mine. "I changed my mind."

"Me too."

"Let's go inside. My . . . my apartment. It's—" His eyes darted between the doors. "—closer."

I drew back a little, meeting his eyes. "Not for drinks?"

Darren grinned. "Not for drinks."

"Lead the way."

He led the way. Into his apartment. Into his living room. Fuck, were we really doing this?

He flipped on the light, and we faced each other again. The smoldering hunger in his eyes matched—might have even surpassed—my own, and I was a heartbeat away from putting him over a stack of boxes or up against the wall again when he nodded toward the hallway. Wordlessly, without touching, we followed the short hall toward his bedroom.

I liked the way he worked: get in the house and go straight to the bedroom. Straight to business.

And the second we were in his bedroom, he was against me. And this time, I was against the wall. Kissing, grinding, grabbing . . .

Wait. Isn't he a . . .

Do ministers do *this?*

Then his lips were on my neck, and my hands were under his shirt, and apparently ministers *did* do this.

We stumbled toward his bed. Somewhere in the kissing and shuffling, our shirts disappeared; one second we were fully dressed, and the next, his chest was hot against mine. Shoes came off, nearly tripping us, but somehow, we both stayed upright.

My leg brushed his bed. I groaned and kissed him harder, the reality of what we were doing finally sinking in.

Darren pulled back. Panting, he looked around, brow furrowed like he was either confused or searching for something. Then, "Condoms. I don't . . ." His gaze drifted over the stacks of boxes, most of which weren't even open yet.

"I have some. Lube too. I can . . . I can go get them."

Darren nodded. "Please do. We're going to need them."

"Don't have to tell me twice." I kissed him quickly, and then pried myself away from him. "Back in a minute."

"I'll be here."

"You'd better be," I growled, and kissed him again. Of course that didn't make it any easier to leave. The light kiss turned into a deeper one. Hands on each other's shoulders, we weren't quite pushing away, weren't quite pulling closer.

Finally, he shoved me back. "Go. Please."

"I'll be right back."

Darren nodded, and I hurried out of his apartment and across the hall, leaving his door open just a crack so it wouldn't lock behind me. Then I moved quickly across the landing and unlocked my own door.

I could've sworn my apartment was tiny, about the size of a postage stamp, but it may as well have been as big as a city block right now. I could not get into my bedroom and back fast enough, damn it. The three strides across my cramped living room felt like they took hours, my cat glaring at me from the back of the couch the whole way.

Darren's a minister. You know that, right?

In the bedroom, I jerked open the nightstand drawer so hard I almost toppled the whole thing.

Not someone you should be getting involved with, Seth.

I quickly righted the lamp and . . . eh, fuck it, the alarm clock could stay between the table and mattress. There were more important things to worry about, like that box of condoms and bottle of lube.

Ministers don't do one-night stands.

I pulled out the box and the bottle, didn't bother shutting the drawer, and hurried back across the hall to Darren's apartment. Funny, his place seemed huge too, the living room getting wider with every step I took.

You really think this is a good idea? He's a—

When I stepped into his bedroom, Darren had already stripped off the rest of his clothes and was waiting for me on the bed.

Gloriously naked. One hand behind his head, the other stroking his very erect and very impressive cock. And he grinned at me like *Well, aren't you going to do something about this?*

Yeah. Don't care what he is. Sex. Now.

I set the condoms and lube on his nightstand, and as I joined him on the bed, he grabbed my belt and pulled me down on top of him.

"Thought you said you weren't usually this aggressive," I murmured against his lips.

"I can be. Sometimes. When I want something." His hand drifted down my side, his light touch making me shiver. "Don't like it?"

"I didn't say that. Please, carry on."

"Don't mind if I do."

He nudged my hip, so I lifted up a little. His hand slid between us, and when it pressed against the crotch of my jeans, I let my head fall beside his. He laughed and pressed a little harder. "Like that?"

"Uh-huh. God . . ."

He moved his other hand, and I raised my hips to give him more room as his fingers found their way to my belt. Resting my weight on one arm, I pulled down my zipper while he unbuckled my belt, and once all of those contraptions were out of the way, Darren slid my jeans and boxers over my hips.

Between the two of us, getting my clothes off should have been easier—faster, anyway—but I couldn't concentrate on even the simplest task while he was kissing me like that. Or stroking my cock when my boxers were just far enough out of the way. Or guiding my hand to his own cock so neither of us had any hands free for disrobing.

Darren pushed my jeans further down, and then dipped his head and kissed my neck, brushing my collarbone with his beard.

"Should we . . . are you . . ." I'd nearly found the ability to speak again, but promptly lost it when Darren nipped my neck. "Fuck . . ."

He squeezed my cock and stroked a little faster. "Should we, what?"

"Isn't there something . . . rules about you doing stuff like . . . stuff like . . . oh God . . ." I thrust into his tight fist even as I tried to speak. "Ministers . . . aren't you guys supposed . . ."

"Seth."

"Hmm?"

"Shut up."

I blinked. "What?"

"You're killing the mood." And then his mouth was over mine, and his hand was moving fucking perfectly, and to hell with whatever I thought I gave a damn about, because *fuck*.

I slid my hand between us and stroked him too, and for the longest time, we just made out and teased each other. Breathing hard. Kissing harder.

"Guess now would . . . now would be a good time to ask," he said between kisses, "if you're a top or a bottom?"

"I'm whatever means we're fucking in the next sixty seconds."

Darren groaned and kissed me again. I stroked him faster; I couldn't even remember the last time I'd been this turned on, and though it took all the restraint I had—not to mention the promise of what was coming—I broke away from him so I could get a condom. He started to protest, but must have figured out what I was doing, because he let me lean toward the nightstand.

I pulled a condom off the strip, but before I could rip the wrapper open, Darren took it from me. He tore it with his teeth. He tossed the wrapper to the side and grinned at me. I thought he might say something witty, or just roll on the condom and be done with it, but instead he reached for me with his other hand, grabbed the back of my neck—Jesus *Christ*, but he was fucking aggressive—and kissed me.

His kiss was both hot and frustrating. He was an amazing kisser, but I also wanted to turn around, get on my hands and knees, and take everything he—

His other hand was on my cock. Then the smooth, vaguely cool condom. I broke the kiss enough to murmur "Oh, God . . ." as Darren rolled the condom on to me.

"In case you hadn't gathered," he said, "I like tops."

Oh. *God*.

"Then you might want to get the lube and turn around," I growled.

Darren shuddered. He reached for the lube, and after he'd poured some onto his hand, he stroked my cock, squeezing through the condom.

"Turn around," I said. "Fuck, man, turn around, I need . . . I need to . . ."

He silenced me with a kiss, and I whimpered against his lips as he kept stroking me, and just about the time I didn't think I could last another second, he broke the kiss and grinned, and we changed positions.

I was horny beyond words, but as I knelt behind him, I stopped. Stopped and just looked. My tattoo artist's brain would usually see a myriad of designs that could be drawn on that pristine, untouched flesh, but all I could see now were solid muscles and angular planes, broad shoulders and narrow hips.

"Seth," he murmured over his shoulder.

"Patience," I said with a grin. I put some lube on my fingers, rested a hand on the small of his back, and let my other hand drift over his hip and between his cheeks. When I pressed in gently with a fingertip, he didn't resist, and took one finger, then two, with minimal pressure.

I slid them deeper. "Like that?"

Groaning softly, he nodded.

I separated my fingers, stretching him carefully, and he leaned back against me. I stilled my hand, and he moved faster, as if to make up for my lack of motion. He rocked back and forth, letting my fingers slide in and out at his own speed. I dug my teeth into my lower lip, barely even letting myself breathe because I was afraid I'd come from this alone. From nothing more than watching Darren fucking himself on my fingers.

"Seth, please . . ." He shuddered, his back arching and his shoulders trembling.

"Getting impatient, are we?" I gritted my teeth to hide my own anticipation.

"Yes." He let his head fall forward. "*Please.*"

"Hmm, well, you did ask nicely." I rested my hand on his hip, and as I pressed my cock against him, we both moaned.

"I'm not going to move," I said. "You decide how fast, and—" I cut myself off with a gasp as he leaned back against me, and a second later, the head of my cock was inside him. Another forward-back motion, and I was almost completely buried in him. "Fuck," I whispered. "Holy fuck . . ."

He rocked back and forth just right, and I was as mesmerized by the sight of him—all shaking and tension and motion—as I was by the sensation of sliding in and out of him.

When he threw his head back and sounded like he almost swore, I couldn't stand another second. I leaned down, resting my hands beside his on the bed. My body weight kept him in place, exactly where I wanted him, and left him with no choice but to take it as I thrust from the hips. Darren turned his head, reached back and grasped my hair, pulling me into another kiss.

His kiss turned me on almost as much as fucking him did. Everything about him turned me on, and how I'd lasted this long at all mystified me.

Then Darren broke the kiss and let his head fall forward again, and the low groan just about put me over the edge.

I sat up. Grabbed his hips. Fucked him. Fucked him *hard*.

"Holy *fuck!*" I roared, and forced myself as deep inside him as I could go. I came hard, my whole body shaking from that powerful orgasm, and I might have even blacked out for a second or two. God damn.

When my vision cleared and I was pretty sure I wouldn't pass out, I steadied myself with a hand on his hip and withdrew. Panting and shaking, I tapped his hip. "Get . . . on your back."

I took off the condom while he changed position. After I threw it away, Darren reached for me, but I gently pushed his hand aside and went down on him.

The second my mouth was on his cock, he inhaled sharply. His fingers combed through my hair, and he muttered something that sounded like he was trying really, *really* hard not to curse. He groaned and tried to push a little deeper into my mouth.

I nudged his thighs apart with my hand. He obediently spread his legs, and gasped as I ran my hand up his inner thigh. When I slid two fingers inside him, his back lifted off the bed.

"Oh . . . wow . . ." His whole body trembled. "That's . . ." His voice trailed off into a whimper. The more I sucked his cock and fucked him with my fingers, the fewer actual words he formed, until he was just moaning.

He gripped my hair tighter. His whole body tensed and his cock stiffened in my mouth a second before he came on my tongue. I kept stroking him inside and out, teasing him until he pushed my head away. Then I let him go and slowly withdrew my fingers.

"Whoa . . ." He shuddered back down to the mattress.

"You're welcome," I said with a grin.

I'd barely gotten up on my knees before Darren reached up and grabbed me. He dragged me down into a demanding kiss, forcing my lips apart with his tongue. Some guys didn't like kissing after a blowjob, but it obviously didn't bother Darren in the slightest. From the way he held onto my hair and my neck, and the way he moaned softly into my kiss, it wouldn't have surprised me if he had us both turned on and ready to go again before too long.

Eventually, though, we separated and collapsed onto the bed.

"Fuck . . ." I wiped some sweat off my forehead. "That was fucking amaz—" I cut myself off and gave him a sheepish look. "Sorry. I, um, hope you don't mind all the cursing."

Darren snorted. "I didn't even notice it, to be honest."

"Oh. Good. Because there was a lot of it."

He chuckled and scrubbed a hand over his face, disheveling some of his hair in the process. "I'll take that as a compliment."

I turned on to my side and propped myself up on one elbow. "So I thought guys in your line of work weren't supposed to . . . you know . . ."

"Be gay?" He grinned. "Or have sex?"

"Well, both." I rested my free hand on his chest. "Or have gay sex, for that matter."

He put his hand over mine. "That's up for debate. But I also wear mixed fibers and have a slight addiction to steamed mussels, so . . ."

"So you're a rebellious minister, then."

He laughed, running his hand up and down my arm. "Not quite. I just think some of what's in the Bible is meant to be taken literally, and some of it's a parable. And a lot has been misinterpreted. I can't say I know any better than the next guy which is which, but I try."

"Wow. I guess I just never put ministers and casual sex in the same sentence."

"It's not usually how I do things." Mirroring me, he turned onto his side and propped himself up on his elbow. "But I'm not feeling terribly guilty about it."

I grinned. "Neither am I, but then, I'm an atheist. No conscience and all of that."

Darren laughed again. "Uh-huh. I'm sure." He put a hand on my chest and drew ticklish circles with his middle finger. "I'm not a priest. We're allowed. The minister at my last church had seven kids, so I'm pretty sure he wasn't celibate either."

"Married, though, right?"

"He can legally *get* married. I can't." Darren shrugged. "And for the record, seven months after his twentieth wedding anniversary, his oldest daughter turned twenty." His eyes narrowed, and that lopsided grin made my pulse go wild. "So, I'm pretty sure I'm not the only man of the cloth who's rather enamored of—" He trailed a fingertip down the center of my chest, drawing a few soft curses out of me. "—temptations of the flesh."

"Is that right?"

"Yep."

I mirrored his gesture, drawing a finger down his chest, but I kept going. "So how much temptation—" I followed the thin line of dark hair below his navel, grinning when he gasped. "—can your flesh handle tonight?"

Darren bit his lip. "I can take whatever you've got."

"Hmm." I kissed him. "Challenge accepted."

CHAPTER 4

Daylight was a bitch. My head wasn't pounding, fortunately, but I could have done with a few more hours of blissfully enjoying all the aches and pains from last night *without* the hefty dose of unfamiliar guilt that accompanied the rising sun. Apparently all it took was a few sunbeams to crack open the *What the fuck did I just do?* and the *This could get awkward.*

But it was just a one-night stand. What the hell? This kind of thing never bothered me. Okay, so he was my neighbor, which meant it would be impossible to avoid each other even if we wanted to, so sleeping with him was about as smart as fucking a roommate. So the awkwardness wasn't terribly surprising, but the guilt was . . . new.

Whatever the reason, that guilty, unsettled feeling had burrowed its way under my skin, and I braced for that moment when Darren and I made morning-after eye contact for the first time.

As I rolled over and we looked at each other, naked and disheveled in the morning light, all that guilt came crashing down in full force. If fucking up was tequila, this was the hangover, pounding home the realization that last night? Yeah. I done fucked up.

It took two, though.

And judging by the upward flick of his eyebrows and the *oh shit* in his tired eyes, I wasn't the only one who'd be wallowing in regret all damned day.

He pushed himself up on to his elbows, then sat all the way up, each motion subtly increasing the distance between us. "Um. We . . ." His fingers tapped rapidly on the sheet covering his knee. "Do you, um, want some coffee?"

"Sure. Yeah."

Not that I wanted to stick around long enough for coffee, but it gave us an excuse to get out of this bed. We parted ways as people do after one-night stands that shouldn't have happened: awkward coffee, mumbled excuses, and a quick escape with noncommittal comments about "later" and "again." We skipped the good-bye kiss too, which only underscored the point that was already much too clear: last night should *not* have happened.

Even if I wasn't completely sure why. One-night stands were fine with me. But . . . neighbors. Two guys who couldn't avoid each other forever. And one was a minister, for fuck's sake. Exactly the kind of person I avoided at all costs, all wrapped up in a body I couldn't resist. Exactly the kind of person I had no business getting involved with unless I wanted to take years' worth of emotional healing about twenty steps backward.

I tried—yeah right—to get my mind off last night and this morning as I showered, poured another gallon or so of coffee down my throat, fed and watered the cat, and headed downstairs to the shop.

There wasn't much to do right off the bat. I kept my workstation immaculate. The waiting area needed just a little tidying—straighten the pile of magazines and portfolios, run through with the broom and dustpan—and the counter and desks were organized already. Not a damned thing to do, and two hours before my first appointment.

I needed something to occupy my restless hands and brain, so I grabbed a clipboard, opened up the ink cabinet, and started counting cups and bottles.

I was about halfway through our stock when the front door opened. I hoped it was an early walk-in, but it was just Lane. "Hey, man."

"Morning," he grumbled, and sipped his coffee. "How's it going?"

"Good. You?"

"Eh."

Typical. I went back to counting.

"Uh, Seth?"

I leaned back and glanced past the open cabinet door. "Hmm?"

Lane eyed me. "You are aware it's Friday, right?"

"Yeah."

He gestured at the cabinet. "We're going to use half of what's in there before you have a chance to order on Monday."

"I know. I know. I just need . . . something to do for a few minutes."

"Dude, we're self-employed," he said, chuckling. "You don't have to look busy."

"No, I just need to *be* busy. Something to"—I tapped my temple with my pen—"keep my mind busy."

"Oh." He furrowed his brow. "Okay. Uh, you all right?"

"Yeah. Yeah. Just a lot on my mind." I checked the clock. It was close to eleven, and we probably wouldn't see any walk-ins for a while, so I set the clipboard aside. "I'm going to go grab lunch. You want me to bring anything back for you?"

"Nah, I'm good. Thanks, though."

"Anytime. Back in an hour."

I didn't head toward the town square like I usually would. Better food down that way, but it was also the route Darren and I had taken last night, and retracing those steps wouldn't do me a bit of good right now.

I got in my truck, backed out of the parking space, and went in the opposite direction, not allowing myself even a glimpse of the familiar street in the rearview. Once I'd turned down the next street, I released a breath and tried to stretch some tension out of my shoulders.

This was ridiculous. It didn't make sense. Something about last night had me sick to my stomach, and . . . *why*? I'd had more one-night stands than I could count—including a few with coworkers, classmates, and close friends—and none of them had bugged me like this.

I tried not to think about it, but how well did that ever work? And the more I thought about it, willingly or otherwise, the worse I felt. My skin crawled. My stomach twisted. Every time I moved, a twinge reminded me of something we'd done, something he'd done, and queasiness mixed with semi-dormant arousal. Like if I went upstairs to my apartment and just gave in and let the memories wash over me, I wasn't sure if I'd get a hard-on or puke.

Or hit something. Because I was pissed, and I couldn't even begin to understand why. At myself? At Darren? Fuck if I knew.

My mind kept wandering back to that moment when I'd casually asked him what kind of work had brought him to Tucker Springs.

I'm a minister.

Maybe that was the problem. It probably had something to do with the awkwardness from him this morning; I couldn't imagine one-night stands with near-strangers of the same sex were encouraged in his profession.

But deep down, something told me I'd still be this conflicted and weirded out even if he'd been all smiling and flirting this morning, and sent me on my way with the promise of a rematch. I hated that I'd let myself get this close to someone like him. I'd very carefully kept my distance from the religious crowd. They were welcome to their beliefs, but once badly bitten, twice extremely shy.

Except he wasn't like the others. And he was hardly the type to ostracize someone for being gay. He was way too good at giving head and getting fucked to have spent much effort shunning gays.

But he was still a Christian. He was still a minister. He not only believed, he preached. He brought others into the fold. He couldn't possibly fathom why I distrusted Christians in general and usually couldn't stomach the idea of being in the same room with a clergyman.

Yet I'd spent the night in the same bed with one. And I'd loved every minute of it. Every fucking minute. Just like I'd enjoyed the hell out of talking to him over a couple of beers. Last night was a perfect first date and first fuck, except for that one tiny little detail, and I . . . I didn't know what to make of it. Any of it.

The only thing that was clear at this point was that last night had been a mistake.

Ink Springs was always open late on Friday nights, and it was quarter to ten by the time Lane and I were locking up the front door. We shot the shit for a few minutes, and then he drove off.

I didn't go upstairs right away. For the longest time, I stood in front of the door leading up to the stairwell. What if Darren was awake? Those walls were so thin I swore I could hear spiders walking through that hallway at night. If he was awake, he'd hear me. And then he might come out. And I wasn't sure if I was more afraid he'd feel as uncomfortable and awkward as I did, or if he'd think nothing at all of what we'd done last night.

I'd find that out when we finally crossed paths again. Obviously he could stomach sex with a man he'd just met. He hadn't batted a fucking eye, at least not until the morning after. And he hadn't been drunk. He'd been perfectly coherent and there hadn't been a trace of whiskey dick in sight, so he'd known damn well what he was doing when he'd kissed me and then suggested going into his apartment.

A minister who was down with casual sex and one-night stands. What the hell?

Whatever. I wasn't ready to face him yet, so I stuffed my keys into my jacket pocket and started down the sidewalk.

Lights Out was only a few blocks away. When I got there, the bouncer checking IDs at the door gave me a nod and let me in without paying the cover. Sometimes knowing the owner of the place really paid off.

Over the music, I shouted, "Jason around?" Of course he was. He was always here when the club was open.

The bouncer pointed at the stairs. "Was in his office last I saw."

"Thanks." I went upstairs and walked right past the Employees Only sign to a short hallway. Then I tapped two knuckles on the door to Jason's office.

"It's open," came the strained, tried reply. I grimaced. Someone was having a rough night.

I pushed open the door. "Hey, man."

He looked up from a mountain of paperwork, and exhaled. "Oh, hey. How's it going?"

"Not bad." I dropped into the folding chair in front of his desk. "What about you?"

"Eh." Jason rubbed his shoulder gingerly and tilted his head to stretch his neck.

"Shoulder acting up?"

He nodded. "I'd have Michael come down, but Dylan's staying at the house this weekend."

"Well, it isn't like you can't have him fix you up in the morning."

"True."

"Must be nice, having a live-in acupuncturist."

Jason flashed me a smug grin. "It has its perks." He closed the thick binder he'd been going through and put his elbow on top of it. "So what brings you here? Out of beer again?"

"Come on, I don't just come down here for the free beer." I leaned against the back of the chair. "Honestly, I don't even want a beer tonight."

Jason sat bolt upright, nearly knocking a cup of pens off his desk. "Dude, what's wrong?"

"Well." I tapped my heel beside the chair leg. "I have a new neighbor."

"Oh yeah? That's right, you were saying Robyn was going to move out."

"She did. And the new guy?" I whistled and shook my head. "Gorgeous."

"Nice! Never hurts to have a little eye candy around the neighborhood." He raised an eyebrow. "So, what's the problem?"

"He's hot, he's amazing, and he's a *minister*."

A laugh burst out of Jason. "Oh, shit. Seriously?"

"Seriously."

"Wow. The fucking irony."

"Tell me about it."

"So, does he know he's living in the gayest part of town?"

I nodded. "Yeah. Totally does. And he's also completely cool with living across the hall from an atheist."

Jason laughed again. "Maybe you're his next project, assuming he likes a challenge."

I tried to laugh, but it probably wasn't very convincing. "Yeah. Maybe." I watched my fingers play with the frayed fake leather on the armrest. "Pretty sure he's okay with the fact that I'm gay, though."

"Well, that's a plus, especially considering what part of town he's living in." Jason shrugged. "What's the big deal, then? So your hot new neighbor's a minister? Just take in the eye candy and skip the religious debates."

Sighing, I leaned back in my chair. "Well, that's a little easier said than done. Especially after, um, last night . . ."

Jason eyed me for a moment. Then he blinked. "Good God, Seth. You two didn't waste any time, did you?"

I laughed, heat rushing into my cheeks. "No, we didn't." I scowled. "And now I feel like shit about it."

"Why?"

"I've been trying to figure that out all day." I tapped my fingers on the armrest. "I guess it . . . I mean . . ." I exhaled hard. "I think it just keeps coming back to the fact that after how things went down with my family and my old church, I don't want to get involved with someone who's part of that crowd."

Jason lowered his chin and raised his eyebrows. "That was one of those extremist churches. Is it really fair to paint an entire religion with *that* brush?"

"Maybe not," I said through gritted teeth. "But the church pariah and disowned son in me are a bit hard-pressed to give a damn about what fucking qualifies as 'fair.'"

"Okay, I can understand that. But you know damn well not everyone with a religious affiliation is like your idiot family. I can see why you're gun-shy, but, Jesus, I would think it would be refreshing to find someone who didn't condemn us the way your family does."

"Maybe it should be, but all I can think is . . . fuck. I don't even know what I'm thinking."

"That his acceptance of who you are—and who *he is*, Seth— invalidates everything that happened to you?"

"I . . ."

I didn't have an answer.

Jason's comments stuck as I walked home from Lights Out an hour and two beers later. I couldn't decide if what he'd said made me feel guiltier about my aversion to people like Darren, or if it had pissed me off because he'd hit the nail on the head and now I knew why last night had bothered me all day.

Maybe Darren's identity and his self-acceptance did invalidate what had happened to me. After all, he's been so dismissive of the idea that homosexuality was a sin. Or that there was anything wrong with what we'd done. It seemed so fucking easy for him to blow off things that other preachers taught with fire and brimstone in their eyes. How could he so easily ignore the very thing my family and church had used to excommunicate me? What did he mean it was up for debate, or that it wasn't such a big deal? I'd lost my entire goddamned family over it. That shit had better be written in blood and carved in stone for everything it had cost me.

Way too much to think about after nothing more than a one-night stand.

At my front door, I pulled out my keys. Right then, a door opened behind me, the sound simultaneously kicking my heartbeat into overdrive and making me cringe.

"Hey." His tone was guarded.

"Hey." I turned around, ready to force a smile and try to get through the awkwardness.

It was funny how the morning light could turn a night of scorching sex into searing hot guilt, but seeing him now had a completely different effect. I'd spent all damned day thinking and fuming and wondering what the fuck had happened and was happening, but it was near impossible to reconcile the smoking hot guy in front of me with the one I'd been biting my nails about. After being away from him, my senses had had a chance to forget about his smile and those disarming eyes.

Hey, Seth? my senses decided to tell me right now. *Your neighbor's fucking hot.*

He slid his hands into his pockets. "Um, so, this morning was a little more awkward than I thought it would be."

"Yeah." I gulped. "I . . . sorry about that."

Darren shrugged. "Isn't your fault. I just figured we should clear the air and all."

"Right. Good idea." I tried not to let my nerves show.

He gestured at his door. "I know it's pretty late, but it you want to come in, I've got a six-pack in the fridge."

Lead me not into temptation . . .

Calling on every bit of restraint I possessed—and that wasn't much—I said, "Maybe we should hold off on the beers, actually." *I probably don't need any more tonight.* "I mean, until we've had a chance to talk."

He exhaled. "Good idea."

And of course, as it always did when two people desperately needed to talk, silence fell. We didn't look at each other. Neither of us said a word for a good minute.

"For what it's worth," he finally said, "I don't regret it."

I should've found some relief in that. Maybe it wasn't such a huge mistake after all. But my gut disagreed.

Darren's brow creased. "I get the feeling you do?" He drew back a little like he was bracing for whatever I'd say.

"I don't know if I regret it, but . . ." I rubbed the back of my neck. "Listen, it's not . . ."

"It's not me, it's you?" he asked with a cautious grin.

I managed a soft laugh. "No. Well, I mean, sort of. Probably the timing more than anything." Good enough excuse as any.

"What do you mean?"

"Basically, I guess I'm just not in a good place to be getting involved with anyone right now." Yep. That worked. Run with it.

Was that disappointment in his expression? Hard to tell, especially when he shrugged it away like it was nothing. "Don't worry about it. I mean, we have to live next door to each other, so I don't want things to be awkward."

"Yeah. Neither do I."

"Well, hey, if you change your mind, you know where to find me." He smiled, and now I was *sure* that had been disappointment a moment ago.

Damn it, didn't anything make this guy mad? Did he have to be so motherfucking easygoing about *everything*? Totally fine with associating with—*sleeping with*—an atheist. Not even batting an eye at me turning him down for a rematch. Standing there so calmly and rationally, not to mention being all brazenly gorgeous and *totally* throwing me off-balance, he obviously had no idea how difficult he was making it for me to stick to my *I really can't do this right now* guns. Inconsiderate bastard.

"Anyway." I gestured at my still-locked door. "It's pretty late. I should get going."

"Yeah, I'd better call it a night myself. Weekends get busy. Good night, Seth."

"Good night."

He extended his hand. Seemed weird to part ways on a friendly handshake after last night, but it was just as well. The more platonic, the better.

Except he didn't let go. Neither did I. Just like last night when things had taken that unexpected turn.

Our eyes met.

His fingers twitched on the back of my hand. Mine did the same on his. Like we were both thinking about using that casual contact to shorten this comfortable-but-not distance to nothing.

"If it makes a difference," he said quietly, "I'm not after anything serious either." His fingers twitched again, but not so subtly. "Not anytime soon."

"Is that right?"

He nodded slowly. His lips tightened like he was resisting—barely—the urge to lick them.

Oh, hell. Who was I kidding?

I tightened my grasp on his hand, and I'd barely pulled before he was against me and had me all wrapped up in a deep, mind-blowing kiss. I'd spent the whole goddamned day telling myself we couldn't do this, but that was an impossible thing to acknowledge or act on when I was touching him like this. Or when he was kissing me like that. Or when he tasted so much like a night that didn't seem so regrettable now.

He broke the kiss and tilted his head back, and I didn't need to be told twice. I dived in and kissed the side of his throat, the underside of his jaw, any hot skin he exposed to me.

"You sure you have to go?" he asked, panting as I kissed my way down his neck.

"Go?" I paused to flick my tongue just above his collar. "Who said anything about going?"

"You . . . you did . . . I . . ." A shiver pressed his body closer to mine. "No one."

I grinned against his neck. "That's what I thought."

His fingers slid through my hair, but then he grabbed it and pulled my head back, and before I'd even gotten past that shock, his lips were against mine. Fucking hell, but aggressive men were my weakness, and nothing turned me on like—

He pushed me up against the wall. I pulled back and looked at him, completely stunned, and he had the most devilish gleam in his eyes in that split second before he kissed me again. And then his hands were on my jeans. My belt. My zipper. *Christ.*

Darren broke the kiss, and I didn't even have time for a half-assed *Is this a good idea?* before he went to his knees.

Both his hand and mouth slid down and up my cock—one creating friction, one slick and hot—and his other hand rested on my hip. I put one hand over his, grasped his hair with the other. Low groans reverberated against my skin, making sure I knew he enjoyed this as much as I did, and my mouth watered at the thought of returning the favor right here in the hallway.

Damn you, Darren, you're making it very hard to—very difficult to tell myself we can't . . . that we can't . . . that . . . oh, sweet Mother of God, keep doing that . . .

"Oh, fuck," I groaned. My eyes rolled back. My knees almost shook right out from under me. My hand hit the wall beside me, and clawed at the wallpapered plaster for some kind of purchase, some kind of *something* to hold on to as I fell apart.

As he stood, he wiped his mouth with the back of his hand. "You still need to leave for the evening?"

"You want me to?" *When did my teeth start chattering?*

"Absolutely not."

"Then no." I wrapped my arms around him. "I don't need to be anywhere."

"Good. Because you're needed in my bedroom."

CHAPTER 5

I f there was anything worse than an awkward morning after, it was two awkward mornings after in a row. Or, well, I assumed that would be the case, but I didn't wait around to find out. When we'd finally exhausted each other around two o'clock in the morning, and the only options remaining were falling asleep or staying awake and talking, I kissed him good-night, put on my jeans, and escaped to my own apartment.

Where I promptly didn't sleep.

Stanley announced his presence with a soft meow, and then climbed onto the bed. He walked across me, as he always did—Christ, I needed to put the little fucker on a diet—before he flopped down beside me. I scratched his ears, which got a quiet purr out of him. For a minute, anyway. Then he got up, moved out of my reach, and curled up again with his back to me. Typical.

While my cat reminded me of my place in the universe, I stared up at the ceiling and couldn't make heads or tails of this situation with Darren.

Okay, so there was no denying the physical attraction. Or the compatibility in bed. Darren was aggressive and demanding, and then turned around and bottomed with a degree of enthusiasm that drove me insane. And he wasn't after anything serious, either.

Question was, what *did* he expect out of this?

And what did *I* expect out of it? Fuck if I knew. All I knew was that I didn't get hung up on guys. I just didn't. But then, I didn't usually fuck someone I had to pass in the hall and on the street every damned day. I probably could've avoided him if he'd been a little more avoidable.

At least this morning, we didn't run into each other during my "commute." Yet another advantage of working downstairs from my apartment: I could get the fuck from one door to the next in no time flat.

And, in theory, use my work to get my mind off Darren, but that didn't turn out to be terribly effective. Cleaning, designing, prepping, tattooing; even those tasks that held my attention couldn't completely erase Darren from my thoughts.

"Hey, Seth?" Lane looked up from the sleeve he was detailing on a Mohawked college kid's forearm. "Don't you have somewhere to be soon?"

"What? Not until—" I glanced at the clock on the wall. "Oh, shit!" I scrambled to my feet and grabbed my coat. "I'm going to be late."

Lane laughed. "Only you could be late for an appointment that's right across the damned street." Shaking his head, he muttered, "Idiot." The kid with the Mohawk laughed, then flinched as Lane continued working.

At least Michael would understand. He certainly knew me—and my habit of losing track of time—well enough. And fortunately these days, he was close by. He'd moved his practice from halfway across town to the vacant space across the street from my shop after he'd moved in with Jason. I had to say, there were worse things in life than your childhood best friend becoming an acupuncturist and opening a clinic across the street from you so he could tend to your every ache and pain.

Then again, those worse things were having all those fucking aches and pains to begin with. Goddamn this aging bullshit.

As I walked into the clinic, I took a deep breath of the mixture of herbs always hanging in the air. That smell alone was enough to unwind some muscles. It was like a promise that relief wasn't far away.

Nathan, the absolutely gorgeous hipster twink who worked as Michael's receptionist, strutted out from the back room. "Oh, hey you! I was just wondering if you'd make it over here."

I smiled. "You know how it is." I pointed at my shop. "Appointments run late."

"Don't I know it." He nodded down the hall and rolled his eyes. "Mr. 'I only need forty-five minutes for each appointment so don't book them for a full hour' back there will learn eventually."

"Yeah, right." I shook my head. "I've known the man since he was a kid. Trust me, he'll never learn."

"I beg your pardon?" Michael came around the corner. "Are you talking trash about me to my employees?"

"Isn't like it's anything he hasn't heard or experienced before."

Nathan smothered a laugh and sat behind his desk. "No comment."

Michael threw him a glare, then beckoned to me. "All right. Dull, rusty needles for you today."

"Promises, promises." I winked at Nathan, he returned it, and I followed Michael.

In one of the rooms toward the end of the hall, I sat on the massage table while Michael took a seat on the rolling stool.

"So," he said. "How's the neck feeling today?"

"Not too bad. Been a little stiff on the right side the last couple of days, though."

"Full schedule this week?"

"One after the other."

"Dumb shit." Michael smacked my knee with his clipboard. "How many times do we have to go over this? If you'd get some more ergonomic equipment like I keep telling you, you wouldn't fuck up your neck every time you have a busy week."

"And I wouldn't be pouring money into your wallet, so back off."

"Mm-hmm." He stood and set the clipboard where he'd been sitting. "Shirt off. Assume the position."

I took off my shirt and shoes, then lay facedown on the table.

Michael gently prodded my neck and upper back, finding all those tense, tender spots like they were visible to him. He tapped in a few needles one at a time. Out of the blue, he asked, "So what's his name?"

I lifted my head. "Beg your pardon?"

Michael raised his eyebrows, then chuckled and focused on the needle in his hand. After he'd tapped it into place, he said, "Do I look like an idiot to you?"

"Is that a rhetorical question?"

"Yeah, yeah, yeah." He opened another needle packet. "How long have we known each other, Seth?"

"I don't know. Like twenty years now, isn't it?"

He positioned the needle just below the base of my neck and tapped it. "And after two damned decades, don't you think I've learned how to tell when some guy's keeping you up at night?"

I said nothing. Forehead pressed against the doughnut pillow, I closed my eyes and tried to will the muscles in my torso to just relax before all this tension counteracted everything I was paying Michael to do.

"Jesus, man." Michael pressed his fingertips into one particularly tense muscle, and I swore through gritted teeth. He put a couple of needles near that spot. "What's his name?"

I swallowed. "Jason tell you about him?"

"No, he hasn't mentioned him."

"I told him the story last night. At the club."

"I see." Another needle into a tender muscle. "Well, he was still asleep when I left this morning, and I haven't had a chance to talk to him. So I guess I get it straight from the horse's mouth?"

"I guess you do." I swallowed. "His name is Darren." I gestured in the general direction of my tattoo shop across the street. "He moved into the apartment across the hall after Robyn moved out."

"What's he like?"

In spite of all my reservations, I couldn't help smiling. "He's a great guy. Funny. Easy to talk to. You know those people you meet and feel like you've known your whole life?"

"Yep. He's one of them?"

"Very much so." I sighed. "Except for the sort of minor detail about him being a fucking minister."

Michael's hands paused as he placed another needle. "A minister?"

"Yeah. You know. Guy who waves the Bible around and—"

"Yes, I know, smartass. So if he's a fucking minister"—Michael tapped another needle into place—"does that mean you're fucking a fucking minister?"

I laughed.

So did he, and playfully smacked my arm. "You dog. Lead him not into temptation."

"Please." I snorted. "I didn't lead him into temptation. He tore off my clothes and led me to—"

Michael laughed again. "Oh. Yeah. And I'm sure you were protesting the whole time."

"I was!"

"Is he hot?"

"Of course he is."

"Then no, you weren't."

I sighed dramatically. "You know me entirely too well."

Michael just snickered.

"Pity he's part of that crowd," I said. "He's a nice guy, but . . . there's no way I can get involved with someone like that."

"He isn't our families, though," Michael said. "Just the fact that you were able to talk to him tells me he's not one of those self-righteous cunts like the people we grew up around. That bunch would've beaten you with Bibles and drowned you in holy water by now." He paused, no doubt eyeing me the way he always did. "Obviously he's not that type, is he?"

"No, he's not."

"Then give him a chance."

I sighed. "With a past like mine, that's easier said than done, don't you think?"

"Maybe. But it could be worth it."

"Yeah. Maybe."

"Well, at least don't write him off quite yet. Now lay here and relax for a while. I'll be back in ten."

He left me in the dark, quiet room, and I closed my eyes as the muscles in my back and neck slowly unwound—as much as they could with Darren still front and center in my mind, of course. Add to that a few aches and twinges to remind me that no, I hadn't imagined last night, and it was difficult to relax. Fortunately, though, the sleepless night caught up with me, and I managed to drift off for a little while.

Eventually, Michael came back in. Neither of us said anything as he took out all the needles, and once he was done with that, I sat up. We discussed my neck and shoulder, same shit we did every other week, but when we were done, he didn't dismiss me.

He folded his hands on top of his clipboard. "While you were in here, I was thinking about your situation. With your neighbor."

"Oh, yeah?"

He nodded. "And I can understand where you're coming from, being hesitant about this guy. I was there, man. I saw what you went through. But . . ." He tapped a pen on the clipboard. "The bullshit our families put us through, especially yours, is a big part of why I didn't accept I was gay myself until fairly recently. And if I had let what happened to both of us keep controlling me, I would have missed out on Jason. Plain and simple."

I gingerly rubbed the back of my neck. "Except this isn't a matter of accepting my sexuality or something like that. I feel like . . . I don't know, like I've suddenly got a crush on the football player who beat me up in school."

"Seth, if anything, you've got a crush on someone who happens to play for the same team as that asshole. Hell, someone who just happens to play the same sport. Doesn't mean he had any part of hurting you, he's just playing football with the guy."

I chewed my lip. "What would you do, then? If Jason were part of the same church our families are part of?"

"Darren *isn't* part of that church," he said. "And obviously he's gay too, so I don't imagine he's going to shun you for it. Quite the opposite, from the sound of it."

I didn't say anything.

"He could be worth it," Michael said after a moment.

"He could be. Or this could blow up in my face. Badly."

"Maybe. Things could have blown up between me and Jason. He was my patient and my roommate, for crying out loud, so believe me, I get it." He cocked his head, arching an eyebrow like he always did when he saw right through me. "I think you're worried because you're afraid you might get attached to him."

I swallowed.

He went on. "I think you're less worried about having a casual fling with your hot minister neighbor than you are about getting attached to your hot minister neighbor."

"When did you become an expert on this shit?"

That fucking eyebrow again. "Since I've been watching your dumb ass trying to rationalize your way out of putting yourself in a position to fall in love with someone?"

"What?" I laughed. "What the hell are—"

He shot me a look that cut me off. "Seth. For crying out loud."

"*What?* Who said anything about falling for the guy?"

Michael sighed heavily. "For as much as you try to be a badass tough guy, everyone and their mother knows you're the sappiest romantic on the planet."

I sat straighter. "I *beg* your pardon?"

"It's true," he said with a half-shrug. "And especially when it comes to this guy."

"Michael, I've known him for like two days. What the hell?"

"Mm-hmm."

I held his gaze, trying to read his expression. "What?"

"Seth." Michael sighed. "I'm not saying you two are destined to fall in love or something, but I think you're jumping the gun by closing yourself off to the possibility. And with this guy in particular, I'm thinking that knee-jerk reaction might be a mistake."

I shifted uncomfortably. "How do you figure?"

"At the beginning of your appointment, I asked you what he was like."

"And?"

"And there were two ways you could have answered that. One was the way you do when you're lusting after someone and couldn't care less if anything goes beyond that. You would have been describing his ass and his shoulders, and saying he had a mouth that was made for something you would describe in some poetically obscene way." Michael's eyebrow quirked. "When I asked you about this guy? You said he was funny and easy to talk to."

My heart dropped. I hadn't even noticed that myself, but of course this motherfucker knew me way too well.

Michael laughed softly. "And don't even try to argue with me. I can tell at a hundred paces when you even think you *might* fall for someone." He rested his elbows on his knees and leaned a little closer. "The weird thing is seeing you fight it this hard."

I lowered my gaze. "I've only known him for a few days."

"Never stopped you before."

I didn't respond.

Michael sighed. "I know the fact that he's a minister makes you nervous. And you *know* I understand why. But if there's something about this guy that's making you sit up and take notice, and you have to fight this hard to convince yourself not to see where things go with him, then maybe he's worth the risk." Before I could answer, he added, "Seth, your parents cost you a lot of good things in your life." He inclined his head, and his expression was serious enough to make my heart stop. "Don't let them cost you this too."

I avoided Michael's gaze. "What happens if it doesn't work out?" I gestured toward my building. "We live across the hall from each other."

Michael shrugged. "So you just quietly pass in the hall like you would with any other shitty neighbor."

I glared at him. "You really think it'd be that simple with an ex?"

"Probably not. But I'm guessing it won't be much less awkward if you guys are just passing in the hall with all this tension and shit between you."

Or if we keep dragging each other to bed, even when it's probably not a good idea. "Fair point."

"Just talk to him, take it a day at a time, and for the love of God, don't fuck this up."

I laughed. "I'll try not to."

"Good. Anyway, I have to get to my other patients. Keep me posted."

"Will do."

"All right. Tell Nathan to set you up two weeks from Monday." Michael picked up his clipboard. "But if it gets too painful, I can get you in sooner. And check into some of that ergonomic equipment, would you?"

"Will do."

"Liar," he muttered.

We both laughed. Then we hugged briefly, and he left the room while I put my shirt and shoes back on.

He was right about Darren. Of course he was. I barely knew Darren, but I could see myself wanting more from him than sex and friendship. We just clicked too well, and I couldn't ignore that. Logically and intellectually, I knew that.

It wasn't the logical and intellectual part of me that was terrified of getting involved with Darren, though. And that part was certain the only way I wasn't getting hurt was if we just stayed friends. No matter how much I wanted him.

CHAPTER 6

Wednesday was one of *those* days. Enough cancellations to put me in the red for the day. Malfunctioning equipment. A moody business partner.

And to top it off, a pissed-off parent threatening to call the cops because I'd tattooed his sixteen-year-old son. Like it was my fault the kid had an absolutely bulletproof fake ID and looked like he was twenty-five. I was damned careful when it came to minors, but I wasn't a fucking psychic.

By the time I finished my last appointment at quarter past seven, I was done. Time for a beer, some mindless television, and an early night. Good thing I didn't have much of a commute, or I'd have been a poster child for road rage.

In fact, as I leaned into the open refrigerator, pondering what might accompany that much-needed cold one, it dawned on me that I was way too fucking wound up for a drink. Alcohol had a tendency to amplify moods like this, and I didn't need that shit tonight. Not when my neck was already tightening up so bad I was half-tempted to ask Michael if he was game for a house call. Maybe he could have a beer, and I could have some acupuncture.

Quiet footsteps passed by my door out in the hall and tightened every already-tense muscle in my upper torso.

A door opened. Closed.

I swallowed.

Darren was home. On the other side of this wall.

I stared at that wall. Tried not to hear the echoes of the nights we'd spent on the other side of it. Or think about how much I'd kill for a rematch.

Because we couldn't do that. Better to stay just friends, I reminded myself. Just friends. I could totally handle that. Couldn't really be much more than that, anyway. Deal-breakers and all of that shit. Even if he was witty. And hot. And intelligent. And fucking amazing in bed. And . . . and . . . fuck.

Just friends. Just. Friends.

Forget booze and acupuncture. After five days of avoiding Darren and going out of my mind because I didn't *want* to avoid him, tonight was one of those nights when I needed something a little stronger.

Before I could talk myself out of it, I grabbed my old gray parka and headed upstairs to the roof. The bricks were still damp from the recent rain, and the night smelled wet. Judging by the slightly pungent ozone in the air, there'd be more rain soon.

Robyn and I had left some lawn chairs up here ages ago, and she'd fortunately had the foresight to cover them with a tarp. I pulled one out, made sure the seat wasn't wet, and set it next to the concrete railing. Then I dragged over the plastic table, set it in front of me, and sat.

As I reached into my coat pocket, I glanced at the door. Al didn't give two shits about what I did when I came up here—he'd even joined me once or twice—as long as I didn't do it in my apartment. The landlord before him would've evicted me in a heartbeat, though. It'd been three years since she'd sold the building to Al, and this was legal now anyway, but I still got paranoid. Old habits died hard.

Once I was sure the old bat wouldn't bust me, I pulled the plastic bag with the paper and the mint tin out of my jacket pocket. My mouth watered as I rolled the joint. Not for the taste of the smoke, but for the relaxation that would follow. I hadn't been this wound up in I didn't know how long, and the need for relief bordered on overwhelming. Desperate times . . .

Once it was lit, I pursed my lips around the end of the joint and sucked in as much smoke as my lungs could handle, inhaling slowly so the burn in my throat wouldn't make me cough. Holding my breath, I leaned back in my chair and rested my head against the railing. When the heat and tightness in my lungs just bordered on unpleasant, I exhaled as slowly as I'd inhaled. The smoke gathered in a thin, gray cloud above my face. When it cleared, I brought the joint up and took another long drag.

I hadn't done this in, I didn't know, a few weeks? Couple of months, maybe? A while, anyway. Long enough that it kicked in fast. I stayed as still as possible while my body floated and my head lightened. Enough? Finish the joint?

Eh, what the hell.

I took one more deep drag, and set the half-smoked joint in the ashtray to smolder while I debated whether or not I was finished with it. Which I mostly was. But whatever.

Closing my eyes, I just flew for a bit. One by one, every muscle in my body relaxed. The tension in my neck eased. The knots in my gut unwound.

Embrace the apathy, Michael had once said when we'd been high as kites in high school.

I wondered if he still smoked. Should invite him up here one of these days. And Jason too. Maybe Darren.

Darren.

Christ.

A shiver worked its way through the haze of *don't give a fuck*. My mind replayed a moment earlier this afternoon when I'd surreptitiously watched him walk past the shop. Head down, hands in his jacket pockets, he'd glanced in the window and smiled *just* long enough to do all kinds of things to my pulse. Even now, lounging in a chair, three tokes to the wind, the memory alone was enough to have the same effect.

Especially when it triggered more memories. The first time I'd seen him. That first kiss that had come out of nowhere. "*I'm not normally so . . .*" "*Aggressive?*" "*Yeah. That. Not with someone I just met.*" "*Well, if it's any consolation, I am.*" The sex. Fuck, the sex. "*In case you hadn't gathered, I like tops.*"

I shivered again. So much for getting my mind off Darren.

Getting high to get my mind off a minister. There was something almost poetic about that. Or maybe I was just high.

I tugged at the front of my jeans to accommodate my hard-on. It occurred to me now that I probably should've taken into consideration the fact that weed didn't just relieve stress: it made me horny as fuck. Usually not such a big deal. In fact, it was kind of the routine: smoke, relax, go back to my apartment, jerk off, kill a bag of Doritos, jerk off again, and then sleep like the dead for a few hours. When I woke up at noon, I'd be a new man. And I'd probably jerk off again.

None of which did a goddamned thing to get my mind off that minister who had set up shop front and center in my brain. Instead of drifting off into the land of Don't Give a Fuck, my mind turned into a nonstop porno, reliving every kiss and thrust. My nerve endings couldn't quite tell the difference between reality and remembering, and erred on the side of making sure I felt the phantom brush of lips or scrape of teeth. My jeans were uncomfortably tight, and if I'd been in my apartment, I'd have resolved that problem by now. Weed up here on the roof, or jerking off down there in my apartment. Need for one outweighed the other. Though if this movie in my head kept going the way it was going, that balance would shift fairly soon.

Door hinges creaked. I jumped as much as the weed would let me, and turned my head.

"Hey, Al, it's just— Darren?" I sat up, wondering why I suddenly felt like a kid who'd been busted misbehaving. Especially as I pulled my parka together across my lap. "Oh. I—" *Crap*.

"Seth? Oh. It's you." He laughed. "Sorry. I, um, I smelled the smoke, and just wanted to make sure some kids hadn't come up here or something."

"Nope. Just me." I cringed inwardly. "Surprise?"

He laughed again. "Didn't realize you were into that, but . . ." He shrugged.

"Eh, I'm an artist and a musician." My turn to shrug, and as I tried to get comfortable with my nerves and this goddamned erection, I added, "What do you expect?"

Darren grinned. "Kind of a cliché, don't you think?"

"Very funny." I gestured at the joint and smirked. "Care to join me?"

I must have been stoned out of my goddamned mind. Completely FUBAR in the head. Because there was no way in hell the Reverend Darren Romero just strolled his fine ass up to my little plastic table and picked up my lighter and that half-smoked joint. No fucking way.

I swore I was getting higher just watching him. Not just the utter shock that he was smoking, but the sheer sexiness of it. The lighter's flame reflecting on his face. His mouth around the joint. His long fingers holding it steady. The way his cheeks hollowed slightly as he pulled in the smoke. Holy fuck. So to speak.

I'd been doing a piss-poor job of getting my mind off him as it was, and he hadn't helped matters by showing up. Now he was taking a hit off the joint that had, so far, just made me hornier, an effect he wasn't doing a damned thing to improve.

Darren turned his head and blew the smoke out one side of his mouth. His eyes flicked toward me through the thin cloud. "What?"

"Um. Well." I laughed. "*That's* definitely not a cliché."

He chuckled. "Not a sin last I checked, either, so . . ." He took another drag.

And I just stared at him, wondering what the fuck was in this weed that was making me hallucinate. It also occurred to me that he'd just taken a second deep hit, and hadn't coughed at all. His eyes weren't even watering. Not much, anyway. Dude had some experience with this shit.

Darren laughed. "Something wrong?"

"Uh, well, no." I cleared my throat. "I just didn't think you'd actually take me up on the offer, and . . ." I trailed off, shaking my head, and it wasn't the marijuana that had killed my ability to form a coherent thought.

I'd left the tarp half draped over the chairs, and Darren took one out from under it. He set it a couple of feet from mine, and took a seat. "You've got the wrong idea about me, Seth." He crushed the remains of the joint in the ashtray. "I'm not a saint."

"Yeah, I'm . . . kind of starting to pick up on that."

He didn't say anything, just closed his eyes for a moment, probably letting himself drift. After a while, he said, "So you're an artist and a musician." He folded his hands across his lap, watching me with heavy-lidded, blissed-out eyes. "What kind of musician?"

"Everything but the employed kind."

Darren laughed. "Could you be a little more specific?"

"Not really," I said. "I've played jazz, grunge, symphonic . . . you name it, I've probably done it."

"What do you play?"

"Bass guitar." I sat a little deeper in my chair, getting comfortable. "Trumpet. Piano."

"You sing?"

"If I want to clear out the house, yeah."

"That bad, huh?"

"Worse. Trust me."

"Well, that makes two of us." Darren shook his head. "I am absolutely *not* a singer."

"We should try out for one of those TV talent shows together," I said. "Do a godawful duet and wind up on the 'Best of the Worst' highlights video."

Darren laughed. "There's an idea."

I just chuckled. "So how in the world did a straightlaced, good ol' boy like you wind up a pothead?"

"I'm not a pothead," he said with as much indignation as someone in his state could muster.

"This isn't your first joint, Reverend."

"No, it's not. But I'm not a pothead."

"Fair enough. Neither am I." I rested my head against the railing. "Okay, so how did you end up smoking pot?"

Darren eyed me. "I grew up in Oklahoma, Seth. What else was I supposed to do?"

My shoulder was unusually heavy when I lifted it in a shrug. "Cow-tipping?"

Our eyes met. He snorted, and we both burst out laughing.

"That doesn't work, by the way," he said.

"What?"

"Cow-tipping. Doesn't work."

"Really? They do that on *MythBusters* or something?"

"Dunno," he said, his voice slightly slurred, "but it definitely doesn't work."

"So you've tried it?"

"Obviously."

"And? What happened?"

"The first time, nothing happened." He snickered. "The second time . . ." Trailing off, he shook his head and laughed. "Well, for starters, we were drunk."

"That couldn't have ended well."

"No, definitely not." He leaned back and gazed up at the night sky. "And we were drunk enough we apparently couldn't tell the difference between a cow and a bull."

My jaw dropped. "No shit?"

Chuckling, he nodded. "If you can imagine the running of the bulls, but with five idiots and one bull in a cow pasture."

"Oh, Jesus. Anybody get hurt?"

"Not seriously," he said. "But I think it traumatized one of my friends."

"Oh, yeah?"

Darren laughed, the sound edging toward that baked giggle that always followed a couple of tokes. "To this day, if you take him into a country bar with a mechanical bull, the poor boy breaks out in a sweat."

I burst out laughing, probably as much from the weed as the comment. "Really? A *mechanical* bull?"

"Yep. Poor guy." Darren could barely speak, he was laughing so hard. "He's in for it when he inherits his dad's cattle ranch."

We looked at each other and doubled over laughing.

It was hard to say how long we spent up there. Weed and time did weird things to each other, so keeping track was difficult. But eventually, after sharing a second joint and telling random stories that were probably not nearly as funny as we both thought they were, we called it a night. I put the mint tin and lighter in my pocket, and we stacked the chairs under the tarp. Then we headed downstairs to our respective apartments.

In the hallway, we stopped. Keys in hands, but not yet in doors.

After almost a full minute, he broke the silence. "Well, thanks for the, um . . ."

"Weed, Darren. It's called weed."

He laughed. "Yes, I'm aware of that. Thank you." He met my eyes, and I very nearly dropped my keys.

We held each other's gazes. My mind, of course, picked that moment to remind me of the first and second nights when a moment like this had led to a kiss that led us into his apartment.

And Darren picked *that* moment, when I'd spaced out for a few seconds, to step closer, and then he had my attention, and he didn't kiss me, and I didn't kiss him, the kiss just fucking happened. Slow, lazy, downright sensual, and hot as hell, lighting up my nerve endings and bringing hundreds of goose bumps to life beneath my clothes.

Through the haze came a single, jarring stroke of clarity: did weed have the same effect on him as it did me?

And even if it didn't have that effect on him, the fact was, it *did* have that effect on me. Which meant there was no way to know where the high ended and the legitimate desire for Darren began. Or if it even fucking mattered, because I wanted him whether I was high or not.

And remember how weird it was after the first time? When there wasn't weed involved?

Wouldn't be any better this time. Worse, in fact. One of us taking advantage of the other after the weed lowered our inhibitions. Though who was taking advantage of whom? Fuck if I knew.

I pulled back. "We shouldn't do this," I whispered. "The . . . the weed. I don't want . . ."

Darren loosened his grasp on my jacket. "You're probably right."

"I know I'm right, but goddamn it, I . . ." I leaned in again.

"Me too," he said, and didn't resist at all when I kissed him. And about the time I convinced myself I should pull away, his fingers ran through my hair, nails grazing my scalp, and I was a lost cause. I pushed him up against the wall. He gripped my hair and the back of my neck. Even over the lingering smoke, I could smell his all-too-familiar scent, and my mind went straight back to that first night. And the second one. The second one that had started when he'd given me a blowjob right out here in the hallway. *Fuck . . .*

You're high, Seth. And so is he.

Somehow, I found the restraint to push myself off him. "Fuck. I'm sorry."

Darren swept his tongue across his lips. "For what?"

"We shouldn't do this. Not after we've, um, been smoking." *We shouldn't do this at all.*

He exhaled, his shoulders dropping a little. "You're right."

I swallowed. "I should go."

"Yeah. I should . . . I . . ." He gestured at his door. "I should turn in for the night."

"Me too."

"Right. Good night, Seth."

I swallowed. "Good night. I'll see you around."

He nodded, and we both turned toward our respective apartments. I unlocked my door and slipped out of the hallway before I could change my mind. His door opened and closed pretty quickly, too.

As soon as I was alone, I leaned against the door and rubbed my vaguely burning eyes. Had I really just turned down a night with Darren? When I was so goddamned horny I couldn't see straight?

But we had a hard enough time making postcoital eye contact when illicit substances weren't involved. No point in making the awkwardness worse, since *that* was something I wouldn't be able to relieve by frantically jerking off in the shower.

Calling it off had been the right thing to do. I knew it was.

But I still had a hard-on.

Which I desperately needed to take care of.

And I would.

Right after I did something about this sudden hankering for Doritos . . .

CHAPTER 7

Surprise, surprise: it took less than twenty-four hours for us to run into each other again. This time, Darren was pulling groceries out of his car while I closed up the shop.

"Hey," I said. "Long time, no see."

Darren chuckled. "Yeah, something like that." He put the handles of another plastic bag over his wrist, grimacing as he did.

"You need a hand with those?" I asked.

He hesitated, then exhaled and set one of the bags down. "You don't mind?"

"Not at all. Give me a second." I locked the studio door, then pocketed my keys and stepped off the curb. "Getting ready for Armageddon?"

"Just finally getting around to actually stocking up the kitchen." He handed me a couple of bags. "You know how it is right after you move."

"No kidding." I smirked as I took another bag off his hands. "And if you're anything like me, you're probably low on snack food after last night."

Darren chuckled and hoisted the last bag out of the trunk before he closed the lid with his elbow. "If we do that again, I'm going to have to permanently evict all the snack food from my apartment."

"Well, if you do, and then we do, I always keep Doritos around just in case."

"I'll keep that in mind."

We took the groceries up to his apartment. He'd definitely settled in since the last time I'd been in here. There were still a few boxes lying around, some open and some still sealed, and about a third of the shelves were bare, but he'd put out a few decorations and hung some pictures. Mostly family photos and a framed print of some music festival's poster.

Naturally, there was a cross on one wall—simple, just plain wood—and a weathered leather-bound Bible on the coffee table between a couple of candles and an Xbox controller. The religious touches didn't surprise me, but they were a constant reminder of why Darren and I were permanently friend-zoned.

We unpacked the dozen or so bags, and after everything was put away, he wadded up the plastic bags and put them in a drawer. Probably to reuse; I did the same thing.

Then he faced me, drumming his fingers on the counter. "Well. I think that's everything. Thanks for your help."

"Anytime."

"While you're here, though . . ." The drumming slowed.

"Hmm?"

"There's something I wanted to ask you about."

My throat tightened. "Okay . . ."

He chewed his lip and fidgeted uncomfortably. My mind came up with all manner of things he might want to talk about—the night we'd smoked, the nights we'd fucked, what to do with tonight—but I wasn't quite ready when he finally blurted out, "I'd like a tattoo."

"Seriously?" I curled my fingers at my side just thinking about tattooing Darren's skin. "What happened to being afraid of needles?"

Darren fidgeted, not quite hiding a shudder. "Well, I'm not crazy about the idea, but a friend drew a design for me a few years ago, and I've been trying to work up the nerve to get it done." He met my eyes. "If you're willing to, I'd like to have you put it on."

"Can, um, can I see the design?"

"Yeah. Sure."

To my surprise, he took me back into the living room and then opened the leather-covered Bible on the coffee table. Inside its cover was a folded piece of paper, which he withdrew and handed to me.

I carefully unfolded it. Though religious designs weren't my cup of tea, this one was beautiful. The cross was about seven inches tall and five across. The arms were almost an inch thick, the entire cross decorated with an intricately detailed black filigree that reminded me of wrought iron. Above the left branch, the word Mark, and below the same branch, 12:31. On the right, Matthew 5:44. My knowledge of Scripture was rusty, and I couldn't quite recall the exact quotes, but they rang a bell somewhere in the back of my mind. A very loud, insistent bell. One that resonated into the pit of my stomach and piqued my curiosity—*why can't I remember these?*—but also made me bite my tongue instead of asking Darren what verses they were.

"This is a gorgeous design," I said.

"Thanks. A ... friend drew it for me." He paused. "My ex, actually."

"Really?" I looked at him, then at the design again. "You really want something your ex designed put on your skin permanently?"

He laughed. "We're still friends. It's okay." When I didn't respond, he added, "Trust me. We were completely amicable. Just realized we were better off as friends." He nodded toward the design. "Any feelings I have tied up in that image have nothing to do with him."

"Oh." I glanced at Darren. "Where do you want it?"

"My back." He tapped just below the base of his neck. "Between my shoulders."

I grinned. "Don't want it on your forearm or something?"

"No, thank you," he said, laughing. "This one is for me. I'd just as soon not have to explain it to the congregation."

"Even if it's a spiritual design?"

"Like I said, this one is for me."

"Fair enough." I scanned the design again. "It might be better to make it slightly larger than this. Maybe, I don't know, fifteen percent bigger?"

His Adam's apple jumped. "Why?"

"So the filigree detailing will be more crisp and distinct. And so the text is easier to read."

"Good point," he said softly. "Sure. Yeah. That'll work. So, how much?"

I shook my head as I folded the paper. "Told you when you moved in. New neighbor discount."

"But, that's a pretty good-sized design. It's—"

"Don't worry about it." I nodded toward the door. "Ready?"

Darren blinked. "I ... right *now?*"

"Why not?" I held up the folded paper. "You said you've been thinking about it for a while. Isn't exactly something impulsive."

"Well, no." He exhaled. "I just hadn't quite ... um ..."

"Hadn't psyched yourself up for it?"

"Yeah. That."

I chuckled. "That's the quickest way to psych yourself *out* of it."

"All right. Then let's do this before I do psych myself out."

We left his apartment and headed down to my shop. As I unlocked the front door, I said, "I should warn you. Tattoos are addictive."

He eyed my arms. "Are they, now?"

"Very."

"Even with the pain?"

I flashed him a grin. "Who says it's in spite of the pain?" His eyebrows jumped, and I laughed. Then I opened the door and waved him in ahead of me. "You'll understand in a few minutes."

He gulped, but went into the dark shop.

I turned the deadbolt and didn't light up the *Open* sign. There wouldn't be a lot of people out this time of night anyway, so I wasn't too worried about attempted walk-ins. I flicked on the light in the back of the shop, leaving the front half dark while pouring plenty of bright light over my workstation.

"So." Darren eyed the vacant chairs. "Where do you want me?"

Upstairs in my—

"Just relax for now. Sit wherever's comfortable." I opened the laptop and turned on the scanner. "I still need to make a stencil."

"Oh. Okay, then." He leaned against the counter.

"And you can fill out the Hold Harmless waiver while I do this." I handed him the form and a pen.

After he'd handed it back with his signature on it, he said, "So how long do you think this will take?"

"Which part?" I went through the motions of scanning the design on autopilot. "The stencil? Or the tattoo?"

"The tattoo."

"Depends on how many times you pass out."

He didn't respond, so I glanced over my shoulder. His eyes were wide and forehead creased.

I laughed. "I'm kidding. Relax. At this size and with the level of detail, figure about an hour and a half."

He gulped. "That long?"

"It won't be as bad as you're thinking it is." I gestured at one of my inked forearms. "Trust me."

"So did you do any of that yourself?" he asked. "Your tattoos, I mean?"

"Some of them." I faced the computer again and continued resizing and adjusting his design while I spoke. "The backs of my arms are a bitch to get to, and I'm not very good at tattooing with my left hand, so I've had other artists work on those. If I ever get around to figuring out what I want for my back piece, I'll have someone else do that too."

"Someone to get those hard-to-reach spots?"

"Basically."

"But you've . . . you've actually done some of it. Yourself."

I nodded. "Yep."

"That must take some serious concentration."

"It's not too bad." I clicked Print and stood to pick up the stencil when it came off the printer. "Really, you start tuning out the pain after a while. The endorphins kick in, and it's not as intense unless it's a really sensitive spot."

I swore Darren lost a little color.

"What qualifies as a sensitive spot?" Then color rushed *back* into his face. "Er, I mean, when it comes to tattooing. I—you know what I mean."

I chuckled. "Anything right over a bone can get a little tender."

"What about . . ." He reached back, eyes losing focus as he prodded below his neck.

"I'm not going to lie," I said. "It might get a bit sensitive when I'm right over your spine."

He shuddered.

"But that spot's really not too bad. Not compared to, say"—I pointed at the underside of my upper arm, which was completely inked—"a place like that."

"That's a sensitive spot?"

I nodded. "Very. Lane doesn't think so, says it barely tickles on him, but I damn near had to chew on a stick while my friend worked on this part."

"That's encouraging."

"You're not getting tattooed there, genius. You'll be fine."

"So you say."

"And you must trust me, or you wouldn't be doing this. Right?"

He held my gaze for a moment. "Fair point."

I inspected the freshly printed stencil. Then I held it out to him. "How's this? It's a little bigger than what you had, and I'll clean up the details as I go, but . . ."

He held it in both hands. Then he nodded and handed it back. "Perfect."

"All right, then. Have a seat." I set the stencil down at my workstation. "Shirt off."

Darren regarded the chair for a moment before he pulled off his jacket and T-shirt. I scooted the massage chair closer to my equipment, and gestured for him to sit with his arms over the back.

"That comfortable?" I asked. "You're going to be sitting there a while, so speak up if it isn't."

"So far, so good." He watched as I gathered some gloves, bandages, and a small tub of Vaseline. "You sure you're not setting up for a medical procedure?"

"To hear the health department tell it," I said as I pulled on my gloves, "that's exactly what I'm doing. This does take a few minutes, but . . . gotta keep it hygienic."

"Makes sense." He quirked an eyebrow. "So I didn't need my shirt off quite yet?"

I glanced at him and grinned. "The artist can't see his canvas until he's ready to paint?"

Darren laughed. "I didn't say that."

"Actually, there is a practical purpose for having you take it off now." I put some Vaseline on the underside of the ink cups so they wouldn't easily tip over after I set them on the paper towel. "It gives you a chance to get used to ambient temperature." I waved a gloved hand at the vent above us. "By the time I get started, you won't have any goose bumps or hypersensitivity from your skin being newly exposed to the air."

"Interesting."

He watched me prep my station, and as I put fresh plastic over the gun, he paled.

Just to keep his mind off the torture device, I said, "I'm curious about something."

He rested his chin on his folded arms, and his eyes kept flicking toward the gun. "Yeah?"

"Now, it's been a while since I've cracked open a Bible, but isn't there something in there about not getting inked?"

"In the same section as everything about eating shellfish, wearing mixed fibers, and shaving, yes."

"And about lying with other men, right?" It came out before I could stop it, and I cringed against the impending awkwardness.

Darren laughed, though. "Yeah, that's in there too. And completely misinterpreted."

"Oh, yeah?"

"Find me an anti-homosexuality quote in Scripture that isn't tied to ritualistic prostitution or ritualistic purity and we'll talk." He raised an eyebrow. "And last I checked, Jesus never said a word about it."

I blinked. "You don't buy into the story of Sodom and Gomorrah either, do you? About it being about people like us?"

Darren wrinkled his nose and shook his head. "Of course not. The people refused to be hospitable to the angels, which was a huge offense. I really don't think you can use a group being punished for trying to gang rape a couple of men as an example of God's disapproval of homosexuality."

I set the gun aside and took a disposable razor from a pack. "Doesn't it bother you that the man who was seen as most righteous and wasn't killed with the others was saved in part because he offered his own daughters to the mob instead?"

Darren grimaced. "I've . . . wrestled with a few of those passages. Women were second-class citizens back then. Property. And . . . a lot of Scripture reflects that. I wouldn't condone that now any more than I'd condone forcing a woman to marry her rapist."

"And yet it's in the Bible."

"I know." As he spoke, he watched the razor in my hand, brow furrowed slightly. "Which is why I strongly believe that Christians should be focusing specifically on the teachings of Christ, not everything else that the Council of Nicaea decided to include in the book for whatever reason."

I raised my eyebrows. "That's . . . not something I've heard from too many ministers."

He shrugged. "Ask a hundred of us a question about the Bible, and you'll get a hundred different interpretations."

"So how do you know your interpretation is the right one?"

"I don't."

"Then why . . . ?"

"You were a believer once, Seth," he said softly and without an ounce of condescension. "Even if you aren't now, you know the answer to that."

"Faith."

He nodded. We held each other's gazes for a moment.

Then I remembered the paper sitting next to my ink cups, and cleared my throat. "Okay, well. We're ready to go." I held up the razor. "You sure about this?"

Darren stared at the razor for a moment, holding his breath. Then he exhaled and nodded. "Let's do this."

I shaved the mostly hairless area where I'd be tattooing. As I did, my knuckles grazed his shoulder blade, and even through the thick latex, his body heat reached my skin. A second later, goose bumps sprang to life all over his back.

Through what sounded like chattering teeth, he said, "Thought you had me take off my shirt to prevent goose bumps."

"It's not . . ." I swallowed. "It's not foolproof."

"Apparently not."

"Are you cold?"

"No. No, I'm . . . I'm not cold."

"Good." *Neither am I.* I cleared my throat. "This might . . . um, be a little cool."

He watched me pick up a stick of deodorant off the workstation table. "What's that for?"

"Helps the stencil transfer." I ran the stick over his skin. Then I pressed the stencil to his skin, smoothed it with my fingers, and peeled away the paper, leaving the design behind. Once I was sure everything was straight and centered, I had him check it in the full-length mirror.

I watched him as he used another smaller mirror so he didn't have to contort to see the tattoo. I should've known he'd be even sexier with ink. Most men were. It didn't even matter that it was still a stencil at this point. There would be a tattoo there by the time I was done. Someone else's design, but my ink. A permanent mark on Darren's body. And even the religious significance didn't detract from how hot it looked on him, like it was a sharp, black focal point meant to draw the eye to his powerful shoulders and the way his upper body tapered down to those narrow hips.

He set the smaller mirror down and faced me again, and I jumped, my cheeks burning because he had to have noticed me staring like a goddamned fool.

"I like it," he said. "Now the fun part, right?"

I grinned. "For me, yes."

His eyes widened.

"Relax." I patted the chair. "I'll test the needle without any ink first. If it's too much, I'll stop."

Darren gave the massage chair a wary look, but after only a moment's hesitation, he took a seat.

I peeled off my gloves and, as I put on a fresh set, looked him up and down. Every muscle from his neck down was visibly tense, pressing against his skin in rigid plains and angles.

"You okay?" I asked.

"You haven't started yet."

"Should I start?"

He shifted a bit, muscles moving but not relaxing. "I'll let you know in a minute."

"I'm going to turn on the needle," I said. "Just so it doesn't freak you out."

He laughed dryly. "Thanks for the warning."

I turned on the equipment. Then, watching him, I slowly pushed the pedal down. When the needle started buzzing in my hand, he shuddered.

I put my other hand on his back, just below his neck. He sucked in a breath. I pretended I wasn't tempted to do the same thing.

Focus, Seth. Be a damned professional.

"There's no ink on the needle," I said softly. "It's going to sting, and it's going to feel a little weird. You ready?"

He nodded slowly.

"Okay. Here we go." I brought the needle up and held it close to his skin, but didn't touch him yet. I watched his neck and shoulder muscles tense, waited until I was sure they were more or less still, and then touched the tip to his skin.

He gasped, but didn't move much.

"You all right?"

He exhaled slowly. "Yeah. I think . . . I think I can handle it."

"I'll just do the outline and text for starters. We can do the filigree later if you want to."

"Better to just do it all at once." His voice was taut, like he was speaking through clenched teeth. "I probably won't have the nerve to come back."

I chuckled and dipped the needle into the cup of black ink. "I heard that from a client last year."

"Oh yeah?"

"Yeah." I brought the needle up again. "Just finished his fourth piece last month."

"Seriously?"

"Yep. All right, we're doing this for real now."

"Ready."

I leaned a little closer, held his skin tight with my left hand, and pressed the needle to the uppermost corner of the cross. He gasped again, tensed, and I thought he might've come as close to cursing as he was capable of, but he didn't tell me to stop.

So I kept going.

I'd put on my share of religious designs. Everything from tiny pentagrams to graphic depictions of the Crucifixion to quotes from the Baghavad Gita. Just three weeks ago, I'd done a back piece of the Flying Spaghetti Monster. Tattoo artists didn't last long if they refused designs of religious significance.

But this was different. Surreal. Like I was literally writing in blood the reasons I couldn't put my hands on him except like this, wrapped in latex and in the name of art and spirituality. The Scripture the tattoo referenced—and damn if I could remember what those verses were—may as well have been *Seth Wheeler, thou shalt not.*

I continued down the left side of the cross, nearing the first corner. My eyes flicked toward the names and numbers on either side of it, and I told myself it was just to make sure I wasn't smearing it with my other hand. Not because I was racking my brain, trying to remember what they really meant. For some reason, I couldn't bring myself to ask.

Darren jumped, grunting quietly.

"Doing okay?"

He nodded.

I put my left hand on his shoulder and squeezed gently. "Still breathing?"

He released a long breath, then pulled in another. "Yeah. Still breathing."

"Keep doing that," I said. "Helps with that whole 'not passing out' thing."

He laughed. "You don't say."

"Handling the pain all right?"

"It's, um, taking some getting used to, but I think I can handle it."

"You're doing fine so far. If you couldn't handle it, I think we'd have stopped already." I dipped the needle again. "So, out of curiosity, what made you become a minister?"

"What made you become a tattoo artist?"

I furrowed my brow at the back of his head. "I . . . it just seemed like what I was good at."

He looked over his shoulder as much as he could without moving. "Like you'd found your calling?"

"Yeah, I . . . I guess." I continued with the left branch of the cross.

"Same deal," he said. "I did some missionary work when I was younger, and by the time I came back I—" He gasped.

"You okay?"

"Yeah. Wow." He slowly relaxed. "Must've hit a nerve or something."

"Yeah, there's a few of those back here."

He laughed. "Very funny."

"So by the time you came back . . . ?"

"Right," he said as I continued working on the tattoo. "I guess I just knew what I was put here to do."

After I'd dabbed away some excess ink with a paper towel, I continued working my way down the underside of the cross's left branch, inching toward the vertical piece. Leaning in close, I watched carefully to be sure I made the corner clean and sharp. Once I was satisfied with that, and had begun the vertical line, I said, "You ever question what you're doing? Or rather, what you believe in?"

Darren was silent. I thought I might've struck a nerve, and not with the tattoo needle this time. I kept working, and he didn't flinch as the needle touched his skin.

"Yes." It had been so long since I'd asked, the answer seemed to come out of the blue. Darren turned his head a little so I could see his face in profile. "I do question what I'm doing and what I believe in."

I dipped the needle again. "But you still believe."

"I do."

Silence fell again. I made it all the way down to the bottom corner of the cross's vertical branch before either of us broke that silence.

When he spoke again, his voice didn't startle me as much as the words.

"You don't talk about your family much."

I winced. "No. No, I don't."

"Touchy subject?"

"Just a bit."

"Do you mind if I ask?" His voice was softer. "If you don't want to discuss it, that's fine. I'm just curious."

Seemed only fair, I supposed. Especially if I ever expected him to understand why things like this cross I was tracing kept me at bay. Well, aside from those times when lust got the best of both of us. And if it got his mind off the pain, then . . .

I focused on the edge of the cross, keeping the line straight and sharp. "I haven't spoken to my family in years. Not since right before I dropped out of college."

"What happened?"

I moistened my lips. "My family has never been accepting of people being gay. I've known that since I was a kid, but I've also known since I was a teenager that I was gay." I paused to dab away some more excess ink. "Kept dating girls just to keep up appearances, but I knew."

"Did anyone else know?"

"Michael. My best friend. His family went to the same church I did, so he knew how scared I was of the secret getting out. Actually, he's here in Tucker Springs now." I dipped the needle in the ink cup again. "Runs the acupuncture clinic across the street."

"Must be nice, having an old friend nearby."

"When you can't go back to your hometown? You'd better believe it." I lifted the gun away, and tilted my neck and rolled my shoulders to pull some stiffness loose, pretending that stiffness was just from working, not the subject matter. "Anyway, so he knew, but no one else did. And he was also the only one who knew that by my senior year, I was a closeted atheist too. I just . . . I didn't believe anymore. I couldn't. No matter how much I wanted to."

I dreaded the barrage of *you need to pray more* and *you have to have faith* that always came from believers. But it didn't come.

"So what happened?" he asked softly.

I started the tattoo again, turning the bottommost corner and working on the lowest horizontal line. "After I left for college—after I came to Tucker Springs—my parents . . . God. Every time I talked to them, they kept asking if I'd met a nice girl yet. You know, dropping hints about wanting me to settle down and get married as soon as possible."

"Ugh, that's aggravating."

"Seriously. Anyway, I was just starting my junior year in college, and decided I couldn't keep lying anymore. So I called my mom." That familiar prickle down my spine raced some equally familiar nausea upward. "And I told her."

"And how did that go?"

"Badly." The word came out as a hollow whisper because I just couldn't put any more energy into it than that. The whole thing had happened years ago, and it still felt fresh and raw every time I talked about it.

"Have you spoken to any of them? Since then, I mean?"

"My older brother and I tried to get back in touch a few years ago." I swallowed. "Exchanged a few emails, talked on the phone once. But . . ." I dabbed at some more ink on his skin. "We just couldn't reconnect."

"That's a shame," he said quietly.

"Yeah. But what can you do?"

He turned his head a little, probably just enough to bring me into his peripheral vision. "You must miss them."

"After what they put me through? No. I can't say I do."

He was quiet, but kept his head turned, and I focused as intently as I could on continuing his tattoo, hoping he'd let the subject drop. I'd heard enough *They're your family* and *You have to try to resolve things with them or you'll regret it someday* to last me until the day I died.

I cringed when he started to speak, but all he said was, "So, um, how does it look?"

My shoulders dropped as I released my breath. "It's, um, good. It looks good. It'll be better once it's healed, but . . ."

Silence. Again.

Darren faced forward again, and cleared his throat. "So what's the weirdest thing you've ever tattooed on someone?"

"The weirdest?" I laughed, hoping my relief wasn't obvious, and pressed the needle to his skin again. "Oh, there've been some strange ones."

"Such as?"

"Well, I had a guy ask me to tattoo his new girlfriend's name over his ex-wife's. One elaborate design right over the top of the old one."

"That's the weirdest one?"

"No." I carefully added a little sharpness to one of the cross's corners. "The weirdest was when he came back two years later and wanted me to ink over *that* one with another woman's name."

"Wow." Darren chuckled. "I can't decide if he's indecisive or too quick to commit."

"Little from column A, little from column B . . ." Satisfied the corner was as sharp as it was going to get, I started on the horizontal line of the right branch. "And then there was the girl who wanted a tramp stamp that said *Abandon All Hope, Ye Who Enter Here*."

"You're serious." He turned his head again, glancing at me. "Someone got that tattooed on. Permanently."

"I swear on my life, it's true."

"Wow." Darren laughed. "There are some strange people in this world."

"Agreed."

We kept the conversation on light, comfortable subjects. As long as we talked, the pain didn't seem to bother him all that much—though I did hit a sensitive spot now and then—and as long as we didn't go back to the topic of religion, I didn't have to think too much about the design and the text I was drawing.

About an hour and a half later, I was finished. I cleaned off the tattoo and had him take a look at it. As I bandaged it, I carefully smoothed the tape, making sure there were no wrinkles or puckering that might get uncomfortable, which was in no way an excuse to run my fingers, gloved or otherwise, across his skin.

"Okay, you're done." I got up and peeled off my gloves. "How does it feel?"

"Burns a bit." He stood. As he put on his shirt, he said, "You were right, it wasn't that bad. Just really"—he locked eyes with mine— "intense."

"Yeah. They sometimes are." I broke eye contact and fumbled for one of the preprinted instruction cards. "Take the bandages off in a few hours. Don't let it dry out." I handed him the card. "Just follow the instructions on here, and it'll heal in about a week."

"Will do." He scanned the card, and then slipped it into his back pocket. "Do you need a hand with anything in here?"

"No, no, I've got it." I nodded toward my workstation. "Just need to clean that up. Won't take but ten minutes." I smiled. "I've got it."

"Okay. Well." He extended his hand. "Thanks again."

"Anytime." I shook his hand, shivering when our palms met without the latex in between. "If you want another one, you know where to find me."

He laughed. "We'll see about that."

We both glanced down, and I realized we hadn't let go of each other's hands yet. We quickly released our grasps and pulled our hands back.

"Anyway." He cleared his throat, a little bit of color blooming in his cheeks. "I should call it a night. Are you sure you don't need any help here?"

"No, no, I'm fine." I nodded toward the door. "You go ahead."

"All right. Have a good one."

"You too."

He paused in the doorway. "Hey, you mentioned a while back that you'd be willing to show me around some of the trails. Up in the mountains. Is that offer still on the table?"

"Um, well . . ." It was tempting, of course, but every time we breathed the same air, I was less and less sure where I stood with him, or if there were signals I should've been reading, or signals I was unintentionally giving off.

Darren smiled. "Just friends, Seth. I'm not asking you out."

"No, of course not." I gave a quiet laugh to hide the mixture of relief and disappointment. "I was just trying to think which trails are worth checking out this time of year. What's your schedule like this weekend?"

"Busy, as always."

"Yeah, same here." I spun my key ring on my finger to give my hand something to do. "Monday?"

"Monday works," he said with a nod.

"Cool. Meet me—well, I guess just come by my place Monday morning."

"Can you give me your address?" he deadpanned. "Not quite sure I remember how to get there."

"Smartass," I muttered. "How does eight sound?"

"I'll be there." He took another step, and was outside the shop. "Have a good night, Seth."

"You too."

I deadbolted the door behind him. For the next ten minutes or so, I focused on cleaning up my workstation. Once everything was put away, I flicked off the lights, locked the shop, and went upstairs. As I stopped in front of my apartment door, the knowledge that Darren was close by—just on the other side of that door a few feet away—prickled from the base of my spine all the way up to my scalp.

I imagined myself walking across the hall, knocking on his door, and asking if he wanted a hand with putting some lotion on that tattoo. And as long as I was back there . . .

No. I actually wasn't in the mood for that. When the hell was I of all people not in the mood for sex? Tonight, apparently. And yet I was still tempted to go over there. Not to suggest we get into bed, though. I just . . . I just wanted to be in the same room with him.

And I also wanted to be on the opposite side of the planet from him. I wanted Monday to get here so we could go hiking, and I hoped to hell a meteor landed in Tucker Springs on Sunday night so I wouldn't have to face a trail and a full day alone with him.

Fuck, I didn't know what I wanted or why.

Shaking my head, I let myself into my apartment. I closed the door and closed my eyes. Tonight had been weirder than any of the evenings we'd spent together, and I couldn't quite put my finger on why. On what it was that had left me more unsettled than any other time with him.

Every time I was anywhere near him, my world made a little less sense. I wasn't sure what to make of a gay minister who smoked pot, had the occasional one-night stand, and now had a tattoo. He flew right in the goddamned face of everything that had fucked up my life a few years ago, and he contradicted every reason I'd kept Christians at arm's length out of self-preservation. Every reason I kept *him* at arm's length.

And my mind kept wandering back to that tattoo. To the simple words and numbers above a not-so-simple filigreed cross: Matthew 5:44. Mark 12:31.

I knew those verses, damn it. I knew them. But no matter how much I ran through all the Scripture I still had memorized—and probably would until the day I died—I couldn't pull up those two.

Finally, I went to one of my bookcases in the living room and pulled the dusty black Bible out from between the Apocrypha and the Qur'an.

I thumbed through it to the book of Matthew, and quickly found the chapter and verse from Darren's tattoo, 5:44. "But I say to you, 'Love your enemies and pray for those who persecute you.'"

Then I turned to Mark and found 12:31. "The second is this, 'You shall love your neighbor as yourself.' There is no other commandment greater than these."

My heart dropped into my feet. I closed the book, set it on the coffee table, and pushed it as far from me as I could. Until my fingertips could barely touch it, never mind put enough pressure on it to gain any more distance. Then I sat back on the couch and just stared at it.

Stanley hopped up on the couch beside me. I petted him as he kneaded the cushion and purred, but I still stared at that damned book.

No wonder I remembered those chapters and verses. They'd clicked in my head, but some subconscious barrier had kept me from joining them to the actual words because I knew them, I knew them well, and it wasn't a memory I could face while I was inking Darren. Or even while I was in the same room with him.

"*It says 'love thy neighbor,' Mom. It doesn't say 'thy straight and approved neighbor.'*"

"*Don't you dare throw Scripture at me, Seth.*"

"*Why the hell not? And isn't there something in there about 'judge not lest ye be judged'?*"

"*It also says to love thy enemy. And I do. But I won't welcome my enemy into my home.*"

"*I'm not your enemy. I'm your son.*"

"*Not anymore.*"

And then there was that click, and to this day, the empty silence on the other end of the phone line still rang in my ears.

I rubbed my eyes with the heels of my hands. Of all the Scripture he could have chosen, he'd picked those two. Of course there'd been dozens of verses thrown around during that long, hellish phone call, any one of which would have stung. But that last one in particular cut straight to the bone.

A sick feeling settled over me, bringing cold sweat to surface above my collar. The venom and disgust from my parents and pastor—all in the name of love and salvation, they'd said—still burned under my skin like it had from the moment I'd whispered the words that had turned my life on its ass:

"*Mom, I'm gay.*"

And somewhere in the thick of things, in the heat of a shouting match over my soul and sexuality, I'd let it slip I was also an atheist.

Apostate. Abomination. *Enemy.*

What they called love . . . wasn't. They hated too much about me to love me. And all because of their interpretation of the Bible, and their beliefs about what God wanted.

I slowly turned my head toward the shared wall between my apartment and Darren's. He wasn't like them. He wore his faith on his sleeve and now on his skin, but I'd never heard a judgmental word slip past his lips. He accepted his own imperfections. He'd smoked with the sinner like Jesus had hung out with the whores.

He was the epitome of a Christian. And the Scripture I'd written on his back was the very foundation of the type of Christianity that wouldn't have cast me out. Maybe that meant it wasn't fair to put every Christian in the same column. I couldn't really lump them all together when the ones who'd hurt me weren't even playing by their own damned rules.

More than that, religious beliefs aside, everything within those two verses and everything I'd seen and heard in the time I'd spent with Darren boiled down to the kind of human being I wanted in my life. The kind of person I could . . .

I swallowed hard and raked my fingers through my hair.

He was the kind of human being I could fall in love with.

And that scared the hell out of me.

CHAPTER 8

A t eight o'clock sharp on Monday morning, Darren knocked on my front door.

"Ready to go?" he asked when I opened it.

"Just about. Come on in." As I shut the door behind him, I said, "Just throwing a few things into a backpack, and I need to feed the cat, and put on my boots. Then I'm ready to roll."

"Speaking of which, will these work?" He pointed at his tennis shoes. "I don't have hiking boots."

"We're not going to be on a terribly technical trail today," I said. "As long as they're comfortable for walking for a few hours."

"They're fine for that."

"Then they should work. If you want to hit up some of the harder trails, I highly recommend coughing up some money for a solid pair of hiking boots."

"Like those?" He nodded toward the pair sitting next to my coffee table.

"Exactly." I sat on the couch and picked up one of the boots. "They're worth the money, believe me."

"I'm sure. A rolled ankle isn't fun even on a flat trail."

"Yeah, well"—I pulled on the boot—"you haven't lived until you've half-carried someone down a mountain with a sprain."

He wrinkled his nose. "I'll pass."

I laughed. "You're not going to carry me down the mountain if I hurt myself?"

"Nope." He gestured at my boots again. "So, lace those up good, and watch your step."

"Hmph." I pulled on my other boot. "See if I call Search and Rescue when you're the one with a jacked-up foot."

Darren rolled his eyes and huffed. "Jeez, Seth. I just said I wouldn't carry you down the mountain. Not calling Search and Rescue?" Clicking his tongue, he shook his head. "That's just cold."

"Damn right." I paused. "By the way, how's that tattoo healing?"

He shifted a little like the tattoo was suddenly irritating him. "Still hurts a little. Starting to itch, though."

"Yeah, that'll happen."

"It's not bad. Definitely not as bad as the first night."

"I would hope not." I paused. "Oh, I almost forgot. I made some sandwiches and got a few bottles of water." As I laced up my boot, I nodded toward the kitchen. "Would you mind grabbing them out of the fridge?"

"Sure." He took a step, but paused. "Oh, hello."

I turned my head, and laughed when I saw Stanley sitting in the middle of the hallway. "Hey. Move it, roadblock."

"He's okay." Darren knelt, holding out his hand. "Hi, kitty."

Stanley glared at him for a moment, but then came toward him. He sniffed Darren's hand—audibly, thanks to his smooshed nose— and then bumped his head against Darren's fingers.

"I think he likes you," I said.

"He seems like a nice cat. I'm assuming his name isn't really Roadblock?"

"No. Stanley."

"Hi, Stanley." Darren petted him, which instantly made him Stanley's best friend in the universe. The cat walked in circles with his tail straight up, purring loudly. "You are friendly, aren't you?"

"Until he earns your trust." I started lacing up my other boot. "He's lucky I don't believe in declawing, I'll tell you."

"Yeah?" Darren laughed.

Stanley flopped over on his back, paws outstretched and belly exposed.

"Oh, don't fall for that," I said. "If you want to keep your hand, I wouldn't."

"Duly noted." To Stanley, Darren said, "I'd like to keep my hand, buddy. Sorry." He scratched behind Stanley's ear, which earned him a swat. Then Stanley got up and stormed away before crouching beside the bookcase, scowling at both of us.

"Told you," I said.

"He's a cat." Darren shrugged. "I wouldn't expect any less. Anyway, I'll go get the sandwiches."

He went into the kitchen, and I exchanged glances with Stanley. I had a soft spot for guys who liked animals. Especially cats. Especially *my* cantankerous, unpredictable cat. Something about a guy who'd talk to an animal, stop and pet it rather than keep walking, just got to me.

Once my boots were on, the cat was fed, and our lunches were in the backpack, we headed out of my apartment. Downstairs, I tossed the backpack behind the driver's seat, we climbed into my truck, and I drove us out of Tucker Springs and up into the foothills just beyond the edge of town.

"So, is there actually a spring?" Darren asked.

"Not one that's worth visiting. My friend calls it Tucker Mud Puddle."

He chuckled. "A bit anticlimactic?"

"Just a bit. The only time it's actually worth seeing is usually when the snowmelt has the river so high, half the trails get washed out. It's cool to see, but not when you have to risk your neck just to get out to it."

"So what *is* worth seeing out there?"

"Depends on what you like." I rested one hand on top of the wheel and the other on the gearshift as the highway wound into the heavily forested hills. "There's some waterfalls, a few historic sites here and there. Stuff like that. I kind of prefer the places where you see more animals."

"Really? I didn't realize you were a critter person."

I smiled. "I think I'm sometimes more of an animal person than a people person."

"I've noticed that about a lot of people who have cats. Something about antisocial creatures being attracted to each other."

"I'm not antisocial," I said with mock indignation. "I just . . . sometimes need to not be around people."

"And instead prefer the company of a creature that also likes to not be around people?"

"Hey, Stanley's friendly." I chuckled at Darren's skeptical expression.

"He's a cat, Seth," he said. "Even the friendly ones have an evil streak."

"Okay, fine, so he's an asshole. But I still like him. Even if he does shed all over everything I own."

Darren laughed.

"And you two seemed to get along pretty well, too," I said. "So there."

"I like animals too, what can I say?"

Yes, I know you do. Bastard.

I tapped my fingers on top of the gearshift. "Well, if you want to see some critters, I know a really good trail."

"Sounds perfect. Lead the way."

About fifteen minutes later, I parked in the gravel lot beside the trailhead. Being a weekday and still a bit early in the year for tourists, there wasn't another car in sight. My favorite hiking conditions: deserted.

I pulled the backpack onto my shoulders, and we started our hike. As the trail sloped gently upward, I said, "This part gets a little technical. If you need some ropes or oxygen tanks—"

"Very funny," he muttered.

We followed the winding, well-worn path into the woods. It wasn't terribly steep, mostly wrapping around the smallish mountain rather than taking us straight to the top. The day was cool but comfortable. Early spring meant some of winter's briskness still stuck around, particularly in the higher altitudes, but we were low enough we didn't encounter any lingering snowpack. If the afternoon got warm, which it likely would, the evergreen canopy would keep us shaded. Perfect weather, as far as I was concerned.

On the way up the trail, we shot the shit about whatever came to mind. Small talk, mostly. Bantering. Sometimes we didn't talk at all. Darren was the kind of hiking partner I liked: he enjoyed carrying on a conversation, but didn't feel the need to fill every silence.

A slight movement caught my eye, and I turned. Then stopped dead and put up a hand for Darren to do the same.

"Hey, check it out," I whispered, pointing through the trees.

Darren craned his neck. "What am I look—*oh*."

On the other side of the ravine, picking their way over some rocks and a fallen tree, were several bighorn sheep. Mostly females, with the smaller, straighter horns, but there was at least one ram sporting an enormous set of those distinctive, curved horns.

"You see a lot of those out here?" Darren asked.

"Oh, they're around, but you won't see them all the time. Last summer, though, I got a picture of a couple of the rams fighting. Cool as shit. Remind me one of these days, and I'll show it to you."

"I'd love to see that," he said.

We watched the sheep for a few more minutes, and as the herd wandered into the woods and out of sight, we continued up the trail.

"Doing okay?" I asked. "Altitude not bothering you?"

Darren laughed. "I'll be fine, thanks. But if you're getting tired, we can slow down."

"Very funny. I was pacing myself for you, plains boy."

"Oh, is *that* why we're going so slow?"

We both laughed, and kept walking.

"Man, it's gorgeous out here," he said after a while. "The scenery's just unbelievable."

"One of my favorite things about Colorado."

"The whole state like this?"

I shook my head. "Head east, and it starts resembling Nebraska as you get close to, well, Nebraska. Much more civilized out here."

"Civilized?" He quirked an eyebrow. "Is that what you call it?"

"What would *you* call it?"

He looked around. "Well, it's . . . bumpier."

I snorted. "Bumpier? Really?"

"Yeah. Oklahoma's nice and smooth." He made a circle with his hand like he was running it over an imaginary flat surface. "Now *that* is civilized."

"Uh-huh. Says the man who was just saying how gorgeous it is out here." I shook my head. "So no mountains anywhere? How did you not go insane in a place like that?"

"Would you believe I didn't see an actual mountain until I was ten?"

My jaw dropped. "Seriously? Dude, I went rock climbing for the first time before I was in first grade."

"Yeah, well, some of us were deprived youth who were forced to live in the flatlands."

"I'll say you were deprived."

"Quite," he said. "So do you still do rock climbing?"

"Not for a good many years, no. It was something I did with my dad and brother, so . . ."

"Oh. Point taken."

"But I might try it again someday." I shrugged. "You know, if I ever find someone willing to dangle off a rock wall by a few ropes."

He laughed. "Well, if you're ever willing to take a novice up there with you, I'd love to give it a try."

"Maybe I will." Our eyes met, and the silence threatened to take an awkward turn, so I gestured up the trail. "There's a place around that bend where we can stop and eat if you're hungry. Couple of picnic tables and all that."

"I could eat."

"Let's go, then."

Fortunately, that was enough to get us back on the path of casual small talk, and we continued up and around the bend to a clearing beside the river. Parks & Recreation had installed a picnic area a decade or so ago, and at first glance, the weathered old tables appeared to have been attacked by termites. On closer inspection, though, all the grooves and holes formed sharper, more deliberate patterns.

I dropped the backpack on top of a few inscriptions about "M.R. was here" and "Casey loves Jordan." We pulled out our lunch and sat on the weathered benches.

As we ate, Darren said, "I have a question for you."

"Yeah?"

"I've always been curious about this, but I think I can ask you without it turning into a nasty argument where one of us eventually tries to drown the other in the river."

Laughing, I unscrewed the cap on my water bottle. "Well, now I'm definitely curious, so go ahead."

"You believe in evolution, yes? The Big Bang? All of that?"

"I do."

"And you were a believer at one time, right?"

I nodded.

He stuffed the empty sandwich bag into the pack. "So back then, when you saw all of this"—he waved a hand at our surroundings—"you believed it was created."

I raised an eyebrow. "Is this where you ask me how can I not believe when there's so much amazing stuff around me?"

Darren laughed. "Well, in a not-so-passive-aggressive way, yes. I'm just curious. I've always believed, but I still want to understand how things look to someone who doesn't. It's hard for me to fathom that any of this happened by accident, you know? Doesn't mean I'm not a believer in the scientific theories; I just don't think things like the Big Bang happened randomly."

"Really?"

He nodded. "I don't see science as discrediting God. I see it as explaining the universe that He made, not one that just randomly came into existence."

I took a drink and set the bottle aside. "I think it's even more amazing that it all happened by chance. The whole planet. Us. All of this." I gestured around us. "The odds were billions to one, but it happened, and for maybe the better part of a century if I'm lucky, I get to be a part of it."

"Interesting." He smiled. "Kind of kills that whole theory that atheists think life is meaningless."

"Just a bit," I said with a quiet laugh. "And I'll admit, I believed that myself, back before I became one. But then I realized it's kind of hard to see something as meaningless when it's finite. When I was a believer, it was all about eternity, and it seemed like this life was just, well, a formality. Something you did before you got to the good part." I faced him. "But when it's all you get, you make damn sure you enjoy the hell out of it."

"Interesting," he said again, more to himself this time.

I took another drink. As I capped the bottle, I said, "While we're on the subject of touchy things that might get one of us drowned in the river, I'm curious about something too."

Darren smirked. "Should we get further away from the river?"

"I'll take my chances."

"Fire away, then."

"You said you've been a believer all your life. Was that an issue when you figured out you were gay?"

"Oh yeah. That was a . . . process." Darren exhaled slowly. "Denial, anger, more denial. Took me a long time to deal with it and realize I couldn't change it, and my family . . ." He whistled and shook his head.

"I'm guessing they didn't take it well."

"Not at all. We were very fundamentalist. Dad was a pastor, and all of us kids were gung ho about doing missionary work. So there was a lot of soul-searching in the Romero household, believe me."

"I can imagine."

"Especially my dad. He was furious. Absolutely furious. In fact, he kicked me out."

"How old were you?"

"Sixteen. He just, he blew a gasket and threw me out. I didn't have a job or a car, so I went and stayed with my aunt." Darren met my eyes. "But would you believe it was my dad who eventually helped me find peace with my beliefs and my sexuality?"

I blinked. "You're kidding."

He shook his head.

"Even after he kicked you out? How?"

"Well, even before I came out and wound up living with my aunt, I'd been really angry about my sexuality for a long time. At myself, mostly, because I felt like I should have been able to overcome it, but I couldn't. Sometimes I was mad at God because I was sure He'd made me this way and then condemned me for it. Which then made me feel guilty and unfaithful, and I'd get angrier and . . ." He waved a hand. "It was just a vicious cycle. But I realized it was who I was, and God wouldn't reject me for that. And then I told my parents and got thrown out."

Darren fell silent. He shifted his gaze toward the scenery for a moment, his eyes distant. Finally, he went on. "One Sunday night, Dad came over to my aunt's house, and he sat me down. I remember being terrified when he told me we needed to talk one-on-one. I was sure he was going to give me an ultimatum. When he sat across from me and put that Bible on the table, I was so, so scared that this was it, and I was about to be disowned."

I swallowed, an all-too-familiar sick feeling burning in my gut. "So what happened?"

"Do you know the parable of the Prodigal Son?"

Oh, yes. I may have been beaten over the head with that one a time or twelve.

I just nodded.

"Dad read that passage to me. And I just felt guiltier and guiltier, like he was trying to tell me I needed to be like the son in the parable, and come beg forgiveness from the family. That if I did, they'd absolutely forgive me, and they'd all celebrate because that would mean the son who they thought was dead—spiritually, anyway—had come back."

Sounds familiar. I scowled, but didn't say anything.

Darren watched the river rolling past. "So then he closed the book. And he got really quiet. So of course I'm sitting there, bracing myself and preparing for the worst." He combed his fingers through his hair. "He said exactly what I thought he would. That he'd thought since the day I came out that I should, and eventually would, repent and beg forgiveness just like the prodigal son. And to this day, I don't know if I was about to do exactly that, or if I was going to fly off the handle and tell him where he could shove that parable, but he . . . I don't know, I just saw something in my dad's eyes that I'd never seen before, and so I didn't say anything. I just waited."

"What did he say?"

"He told me he'd been called to that part of the Scripture when he'd prayed after I came out, and he hadn't realized until that night that *he* was the one in the role of the prodigal son."

I blinked. "What?"

Darren swept his tongue across his lips but didn't turn toward me. "He said he preached to his congregation every Sunday about being like Christ, but Christ had never said a word about homosexuality. Yeah, there's some stuff in the Bible that can be interpreted as antihomosexual, but nothing from Jesus. For that matter, He'd never advocated turning away a son." Once again, he fell silent, closing his eyes for a moment. Maybe he was praying, maybe collecting himself. Maybe both. It was impossible to say.

Then he sniffed sharply and wiped at his eyes before he looked at me. "He told me he'd realized that morning, while he was getting ready for his sermon, that he couldn't stand up there in front of all those people and tell them how to be like Christ when he'd put out his own son." Darren swallowed hard. "He told me he loved me. And he asked me if after what he'd done, he had any right to hope he would be welcome in my life again. Like the prodigal son was when he returned to his father."

"Wow," I said.

"Yeah." Darren shook some tension out of his shoulders. "That was the day I realized what I wanted to do with my life. I'd wanted to be a missionary already, even while I was still struggling to reconcile my sexuality with my beliefs, but I just knew right then that *this* was my calling."

"And things with your family?" I asked. "They've been fine ever since?"

Darren shrugged. "There were some bumps in the road. Chris and my sisters took a while to come around. Mom was a little weird when I actually started dating guys. Dad had his moments. It took them all a long time to accept that I wasn't going to change, and even longer that I didn't *need* to change, but we all got it together after a couple of years."

"Good to hear," I said, watching the river instead of Darren.

"I don't, um—" He paused, clearing his throat. "I haven't told many people about that."

I turned toward him again. "Oh. I, uh, hope I wasn't stepping on a raw nerve."

"Not really. It's just not something I talk about except with close friends." He met my eyes. "Really close friends."

My breath caught. "Oh," was all I could say.

He held my gaze. I held his.

My heart beat faster.

Oh God, let's not ruin today with one of those awkward "we need to stay friends" conversations.

Then Darren abruptly broke eye contact and nodded toward the trail. "We should, um, keep moving. Only so much daylight left."

"Right. Yeah. Good idea." I stood and put my water bottle into the pack. "Ready?"

"Yeah." His eyes met mine again. I thought for sure we were going to give in and have that awkward moment after all, but for the second time, he was the one to break eye contact.

I pulled on the pack, and we started down the trail. It didn't take long for us to get back into our bantering groove, and as near as I could tell, he'd forgotten about the tense, slightly awkward moment we'd shared. I sure as fuck hadn't.

I just didn't know what to make of it.

CHAPTER 9

The shop was empty on Thursday night, as it often was, but we'd had some pretty good walk-ins early in the day, so I couldn't complain. A little downtime was good. Gave me a chance to clean, sketch, and totally *not* think about Monday's hike like I'd been doing all week.

I sat up to stretch a kink out of my neck after hunching over a drawing for half an hour. Lane was standing at the counter, skimming over the appointment book. I was just about to suggest we close up the shop early, since things were quiet, when he did a double take at something on the left side of the book. Then he rolled his eyes and turned the page with more force than necessary.

"What?" I asked.

"Nothing," he muttered. "Just noticed one of your appointments next week."

"What about it?"

He glared at me, but said nothing. The typical Lane expression that meant *read between the lines, asshole*. I mentally ran through my schedule for the next week, trying to think what I could have possibly—

Oh.

I groaned and sat back in my chair, pushing away the sketch I'd been working on. "Dude, seriously? This again?" I was so not in the mood for this shit. Not after being up all night thinking about Darren. Again.

He glared at me. "Yes, this again."

"For fuck's sake, man. There's no reason it should be an issue for me to work on him. Do you have any idea how many of *your* clients are HIV or Hep positive?"

He shifted his weight. "None of them have said—"

"Do you make them bring in documentation showing recent negatives?"

"No," Lane growled. "I don't."

"Then who's to say you're not inking people who are positive for either one?" I pushed myself up out of my chair. "At least I *know* this guy is positive."

"Yeah?" He watched me get up and cross the shop as he said, "And I haven't seen you do fuck all in the way of taking extra precautions when you're working on him."

I raised an eyebrow, then leaned down to riffle through a drawer for some pencils. "I take the same precautions with him as I do with any other goddamned client"—I withdrew the pencils and slammed the drawer—"because I tattoo *all* of my clients with the assumption they have HIV or Hep. Don't you?"

"Of course I do. But that's . . ." He fidgeted again, tightening his arms across his chest.

"Lane, think about it. I do the same thing with him as I do with any other client." I dropped the pencils beside my sketchpad and ticked off the points on my fingers. "I wear gloves. I sanitize everything. I use new, sterile ink cups and fresh ink that's never been touched and will never be used on anyone else. Just like I would do with anyone else because I assume—just like you should be assuming—that anyone who walks through that door could be positive."

"Still, I'm just not comfortable with word getting around that we tattoo people who are positive." He pointed sharply at my workstation. "Or you inking them with the same gear you use on everyone else."

"You're serious. We sterilize the hell out of everything we own, above and beyond the state regulations, and you still want me to get an entire set of equipment just for using on those clients."

"What would it hurt?"

"*Lane.*" I gestured at the room around us. "Where would we put extra equipment? Seriously. If we had the space, we'd have brought in another artist fucking *ages* ago."

"We can't afford an extra artist in here, even if we had room."

"Ditto with the equipment."

"Don't you think it's more important to—"

"I'm not going to keep going around and around about this, dude. If you want me to schedule him when you're not here, I will." Muttering, I added, "God forbid I expose you to a leper."

Lane grumbled something I didn't understand, and for the sake of us not coming to blows around all this expensive equipment, I didn't ask him to repeat it. I was tired of this same old argument, and there was no point in dragging it out again.

I rubbed my eyes. One of these days, we'd settle this dispute. Hopefully out of earshot of our clientele.

Right about then, fortunately, the front door opened. I glanced at it, then did a double take.

A kid who couldn't have been more than sixteen sauntered in. Lip pierced, eyebrow pierced, hair bleached. Punk shirt and torn jeans. Radiating attitude from every adolescent pore on his broken-out face.

I saw kids like that in here all the time, so he wasn't the reason I did the double take.

"Something wrong?" Darren asked as the door banged shut behind him.

"Uh, no, I . . ." *Didn't expect to see you tonight.* I shook my head and moved toward the counter. "Just wasn't expecting you." *And I'm not sure how to breathe around you right now.* "How is the, um, is the tattoo still healing okay?"

"Feels fine," he said. "Itches a little."

"That's normal."

"Yeah, that's what the card said. And, actually, that tattoo is the reason I'm here." His eyes darted toward the kid he'd brought in. "This is Max. He saw the tattoo through my T-shirt, and now he wants one."

My head snapped toward him so fast I damn near broke my neck. "And he's how old?"

Darren's cheeks colored a little. "Um, sixteen."

My jaw dropped. "You want me to tattoo a kid who—"

"He's going to get one anyway," Darren shot back. "I brought him here because at least then I can be sure he's getting it at a clean, reputable place."

"And no clean, reputable place is going to tattoo a sixteen-year-old without his parents' permission."

"He's emancipated. He doesn't *need* his parents' permission."

I let my head fall forward. "You're killing me here, Darren." I raked a hand through my hair. "Jesus. He . . . he's just a kid!"

"I know. And I'm sorry. I know this is putting you in a bad spot." He nodded toward Max. "But he's got emancipation papers. For all intents and purposes, he's an adult, which means you're not liable for—"

"It's not the legality I'm concerned about. Eighteen-year-olds are impulsive when it comes to ink." I glanced at Max. "But *sixteen?*"

"What choice do I have?" It sounded more like a plea than a question. "He wants one. He's determined to get one. There's no way I can stop him, so I'm bringing him to you to make sure he at least gets it done safely."

I silently watched the kid for a moment. There were plenty of shady artists in this town. In any town.

"Please, Seth," Darren said, almost whispering.

I gnawed the inside of my cheek, and finally nodded. "Okay. Fine."

Darren exhaled. "Thank you. I owe you big time."

"Don't worry about it."

I came around the counter and approached the kid. He had his arms folded across his chest, and his brow was furrowed as he scanned the art on the walls.

"See anything you like?" I asked.

"Eh," he said with a half-shrug. "It's not bad."

"Thanks."

He sniffed derisively, and his gaze slid toward me. "This all you got?"

"Depends. What do you have in mind?"

"Something tribal."

I eyed his stringy bleached hair and very nonnative blue eyes. "Which tribe?"

"I dunno." He shrugged. "Whatever."

I arched an eyebrow at Darren in what I hoped came across as a loud and clear *What the fuck, dude?*

He shrugged apologetically, but didn't say anything.

I turned to the kid again. "Let's check out some designs. See if anything catches your eye. Come on over here."

I led him back to the counter, and then I went around behind it. I pulled the tribal portfolio off the shelf and let it thud heavily on the counter. "Here you go. All our tribal work."

Max muttered something and pulled the portfolio toward him. He flipped it open and thumbed through it with all the interest of someone reading a book of tax codes.

"While you're doing that," I said, "do you have a copy of your emancipation?"

Without looking up, he dug the wrinkled and folded paper out of his jacket pocket.

"How about some ID to go with it?"

He huffed as only a teenager could huff, then pulled out a wallet that had both a Velcro flap and a chain. Then he smacked a state ID down on the counter.

While he went through the portfolio, I photocopied the documents. I gave him back the originals and slipped the copies into a folder, which I'd file later. Even if he didn't get any ink, that shit stayed here just in case anyone ever asked questions.

"I want this one." He tapped a wide tribal armband. "All the way around my arm."

"All right." I put the consent form and Hold Harmless waiver on the counter. "Read that over and sign at the bottom."

"What's this for?" He glared at me. "I already gave you my ID and stuff."

"Yeah. And this is the Hold Harmless."

He rolled his eyes. "This is way too much paperwork. I want a tattoo, not a car."

"And I want to stay in business long enough to retire as something other than a bum." I pointed at the form. "No ink on there? No ink on you."

"Why? I know what I want."

"Yeah, but how do I know you won't sue me if it gets infected, or you wind up with hepatitis?" I gestured at the form. "I close in an hour, buddy. You want any ink tonight, read it and sign it."

"Max," Darren said to the kid. "This all means he's running a responsible, safe shop. That's why I brought you here. Just fill out the forms."

"This is the guy that did yours, right?" Max asked.

Darren nodded. "Yeah, he did. And I had to fill out the same form."

The kid sighed, but then started reading the form.

I turned to Darren again. He gave another apologetic shrug. He had to know as well as I did that this kid was nowhere near mature enough to get inked, and he sure as shit hadn't given nearly enough consideration to his design.

"Here." The kid slapped the paper on to the counter. "Now can we do this?"

"Ready when you are. Have a seat."

He followed me to my workstation behind the counter. His sleeve was loose enough and the desired location low enough I just pushed up his sleeve and clipped it into place. Then I prepped his skin and put on the stencil.

Once the stencil was on, I pointed at the mirror. "Go take a look. Make sure it's exactly where you want it."

He got up and went to the mirror. Grinning at his reflection, he said, "Yeah. Yeah, that's what I want."

"Before we get started," I said, "why don't we see if you can handle the pain?"

Max laughed. "It ain't that bad."

"Isn't it?"

He smirked at my sleeve. "If it is, then you're an idiot."

"Or I just have a higher pain tolerance than most."

He turned toward Darren. "Yours wasn't bad, was it?"

Darren shrugged. "I told you it was pretty intense."

Our eyes met briefly. His face colored a little, and I shifted my attention back to getting my equipment ready. Yeah, his tattoo had been intense, but the pain had nothing to do with it.

"Whatever." Max sniffed derisively again. "I can take it." He gestured at the piercings on his face. "Bring it on."

"All right." I picked up the needle and turned it on. "No ink this time. Just seeing how well you handle the pain."

"Whatever, man."

I resisted the urge to roll my eyes as I brought the needle up to the inside of his upper arm, ready to press the tip against his skin. He wasn't the first invincible punk to come wandering into my shop, and he wouldn't be the last. He also wouldn't be the first to run out crying, which I predicted in *three . . . two . . .*

"*Ow!*" he shrieked.

One, motherfucker.

He recoiled, pressing his arm to his side like a broken wing and holding up his other hand.

I held up the needle, which was still buzzing. "Ready for the ink?"

"No!" He pulled back even farther. "No, I, um . . ." He snatched the clips off his shirt and smoothed his sleeve over the stencil. "Forget it. I changed my mind. I don't want it."

"You sure?" I asked.

"*Yes.*" He flew up out of the chair and backed away from me. "Let's get out of here," he muttered to Darren.

Darren didn't say a word. He just followed the kid toward the door. On the way, though, he turned back and mouthed, "Thank you."

I just shook my head and laughed.

As I was closing the shop, Darren pulled in and parked next to my truck. My heart sped up as his engine quieted down.

He opened the car door. "Hey. Um, I wanted to say thanks again. For earlier."

"No problem," I said. "So did you really think I was going to tattoo him?"

"Well, I didn't know what choice you had." He stepped on to the curb beside me. "Sorry I put you in that position, though."

"Nah, don't worry about it." I opened the door to the stairwell and gestured for him to go ahead. "Probably better you brought him to me than some of the shady artists in town."

"That's why I did it."

"So, where did you run into this kid, anyway?"

"My church has an outreach program for LGBT kids who've been thrown out of their homes."

My heart flipped over. "They have a . . . *really?*"

He stopped at the top of the stairs, moving aside so I had room to join him in the hall. "Yeah. That's why they hired me in the first place. They needed a youth pastor, but also someone to run the program.

Max is one of the homeless kids who's staying with us until he gets himself together."

"So . . . the church. It actually has a program for queer kids?"

Darren nodded. "The pastor started the program when he started the church. Lost his brother after their parents threw him out, and decided it was his calling to help others in the same predicament."

"Wow. That's . . . um, that's awesome. I mean, that you and the pastor are doing all of that." *Which is not helping my resolve to not want you, right?*

"It's a good program," he said. "We're trying to get some more community support, but it's a start."

"That's great."

Our eyes met, and locked, just like they often did when we were in this hallway. Judging by past experiences, now we were in serious danger of talking about things other than his church's program, so I quickly—and awkwardly—said, "Well, I won't keep you. It's late enough as it is."

He smiled. "Good night."

"Good night."

He started toward his apartment and I started toward mine, but I hesitated.

"Hey, um." I cleared my throat. "I know we don't necessarily see eye to eye on beliefs, but that . . . that outreach program." I paused. "Is there any way I can help? You know, help the kids out?"

"We need all the help we can get." As he pulled his keys out of his pocket, he turned toward me again. "Do you have any evenings off coming up?"

"Monday and Tuesday."

"Why don't you come by on Monday, then? If you don't have anything else going on? The youth group usually helps out on Wednesday nights, but the other nights can get a little thinly staffed."

"I can be there Monday, yeah."

"Great." He smiled. "I really appreciate it. Thanks."

"Anytime."

CHAPTER 10

I'd sworn up and down for the last several years that I'd never set foot in a church again, but here I was, walking through the front door of the New Light Church. On the way across the threshold, I was strangely tempted to stop and cross myself. Very weird for a non-spiritual person who'd never been Catholic, but going into a place like this, I'd take all the wards and protections I could get.

Relax. It's just a church. And it's not that *church.*

So like a vampire strolling onto holy ground, I walked inside.

This definitely wasn't one of those gaudy mega-churches like the one my family had attended. No multimillion-dollar facility. No gilded statues and candle holders in front of massive speakers. No elaborate stained glass or giant screens at the front of a sanctuary with stadium seating and surround sound.

It was almost like a glorified community center. I half-expected the sanctuary to be full of folding chairs instead of pews, but it did have pews. Weathered ones with the odd crack or stain, but pews.

Though it was nothing like the church I'd attended eons ago, it had its familiar points. A black-covered, gold-embossed Bible. Uniform hymnals with their red-edged pages. The odd painting of a pensive, Caucasian Christ.

All those familiar things and the single large wooden cross at the front of the sanctuary were like a weird connection between what I'd believed back then and what I believed now. The memory of my feelings about that icon—the sense of peace and devotion—was crystal clear, but somehow disconnected. Like I'd picked up the emotional memories of someone else. Someone who would never in a million years wonder how anyone could find peace in a symbol akin to a hangman's noose.

"Seth?"

I shook my head, and then turned toward the sound of Darren's voice.

He raised his eyebrows. "You okay?"

"Yeah." I rolled my shoulders under my hoodie, pretending I didn't feel like I was breaking out in hives. "Just, um . . ." *And how exactly do I explain this?*

"There's no holy water," he said. "So you shouldn't have to worry about it bubbling or frothing when you walk by."

I laughed. "Well, that's always a plus."

He chuckled, but his brow was still creased. "You sure you're okay?"

I swallowed. "I'm fine. It's just a little surreal to be back in a church after so long." A little surreal? Understatement.

"I don't doubt it," he said. "If you're sure you're all right, though, I'll show you around."

"Right. Sure." I followed him further into the church.

"There isn't really much to it. The classrooms behind the sanctuary have been converted into dorms. The pastor and his wife live in the apartment over there"—he nodded toward the left side of the sanctuary—"and volunteers stay here in shifts so there's also at least two people over eighteen in the building. And in about—" he checked his watch "—thirty minutes, the other volunteers will be here to start getting dinner put together for the kids. After they've eaten, it can be anything from helping them study or apply for colleges to playing dodge ball in the sanctuary."

"Dodge ball?" I blinked. "In the sanctuary?"

"What? You're not afraid to play against a bunch of kids, are you?"

"Pfft. I'll wipe the floor with them."

Darren flashed me a grin. "I'll remember that when I'm helping you ice a black eye at the end of the night."

I laughed. "Yeah. We'll see about that."

Chuckling, he gestured for me to follow him. "All right, let's put you to work before you get into trouble."

"It's almost frightening how well you seem to know me."

He just grinned. And I shoved all my thoughts about how well *I* wanted to know *him* to the back of my mind.

He took me back and introduced me to some of the kids who were staying in the church's makeshift dorm. That was eerie and more than a little disturbing, seeing all these kids—mostly sixteen or seventeen, one who couldn't have been more than thirteen—essentially homeless and turned out on their own. There had been many times over the last several years when I was thankful I'd dodged that bullet, that when my family had disowned me, I'd been an adult with the capability of getting on my feet, even if it took some struggling. This was one of those times.

As everyone started migrating from the dorms toward the kitchens, I noticed one kid sitting off to the side in the sanctuary, refusing to acknowledge anyone else and making no move to join everyone. Her hair was pulled back in a ponytail, and her blouse sat on shoulders that—

Wait.

The shape of the shoulders. The lack of shape in the hips. Makeup covering a jawline that was coarser than I'd have expected. My heart sank. At this age, most boys pined for that time when they could justify shaving more than once or twice a week. This poor girl was well ahead of that curve.

I turned to Darren, and gestured at the girl. "Hey, is she okay?"

He sighed. "Sometimes it takes a while for kids to feel like they're part of the group. She's the only trans girl here right now, and I think she's self-conscious about her voice."

"Her voice?"

"You think it sucked when we were teenagers and our voices kept cracking?" He nodded toward her. "Think how that must be for her."

I grimaced. "Poor kid."

"No kidding."

I looked over at the kids heading into the kitchen. Then at the girl sitting by herself. "Listen, um, can you do without me for a few minutes?"

Darren turned to me and shrugged. "Yeah, sure. Why?"

"I'm going to see if I can talk to her."

"Good luck," Darren said without a trace of sarcasm. "I've tried, but..."

"Couldn't hurt to try."

He followed the other kids, and I walked back to where the girl sat alone. As I approached her, I said, "Hi," silently cursing my own awkwardness.

No response.

I sat beside her, but kept a comfortable foot or so between us. "You all right? You're awfully quiet."

She turned away, and I cringed on her behalf when her Adam's apple jumped.

"What's your name?" I asked.

She glared at me, and pointed at the name tag on her blouse.

"Josephine." I extended my hand. "I'm Seth."

She didn't take my hand, and instead turned her head away again.

I chewed my lip. "You know, there's—"

"I don't want to talk to anyone, all right?" she snapped, her cheeks immediately reddening under her makeup. Darren was right: her voice was caught in that limbo between a boy's and a woman's, not quite out of the higher register of the former but trying really hard to dip into a register that was too low for the latter. Nothing sabotaged an attempt to master a female speaking voice like that bitch called puberty.

Josephine clenched her jaw.

"Listen, um . . ." I cleared my throat. "I might be able to help you with your voice."

She didn't speak.

"There's a vocal teacher at Tucker U," I said. "She can work with you."

"I don't want to learn to sing," she growled. "I just want to talk without—" Her voice cracked, and she made a frustrated gesture at her throat.

I nodded. "Yeah, but she can help you learn control."

Josephine's brow furrowed, but the tension in her shoulders lessened. "Does that . . . does that work?"

"It helps." I smiled. "A friend of mine took singing lessons when she was transitioning, and wound up the lead singer in a metal band."

For the first time since I'd seen her, some of the hostility lessened in Josephine's expression. "Really?"

"Yep. She was damn good. And she could turn around and nail some of the lower notes, which made her an amazing musician."

"And she . . ." Josephine hesitated, shifting a little so she was facing me. "She passed? For a girl, I mean?"

"To be honest, I didn't even know she was born male until a good six months after I joined her band."

She wrinkled her nose. "You're in a band?" Then she eyed at my arms. "I guess you do kind of fit the part."

I laughed. "Should I take that as a compliment?"

She managed a laugh too, even if it was quiet. "So, what? Are you in one of those Christian metal bands or something?"

"Uh, no." I chuckled. "I don't think they'd let me stay in a Christian band for very long."

"Why not?"

"Because a prerequisite for a band like that is—" My teeth snapped shut as I remembered, a little too late, where I was. "Um, well . . ."

"I thought the only prerequisite was you had to be a crappy musician."

I laughed. "Well, okay, there's that. But you also have to be a Christian."

Josephine blinked. "You're . . . not?"

I shook my head. "I'm an atheist. Have been for a long time."

"Oh, yeah?" She looked up at me. "Then why are you here?"

"Because what happened to you and half the kids here," I said, "happened to me."

"It did?"

I nodded. "My parents found out I was gay, and they disowned me."

"But this is a church."

"I know. But Darren—Pastor Romero, I mean—and I are friends." Just friends. Just. Friends. "He said they needed some help down here, so . . ."

"Oh." She was quiet for a moment. "So your parents really disowned you, too?"

I nodded. "Haven't spoken to them in years."

"What happened?"

I forced back the sick feeling that always came with rehashing this story. "I grew up in Los Angeles. My parents were hardcore Christian. Like . . . hardcore. So I was raised that way, and it was one of those crazy extremist churches. Nothing like this." I waved a hand at our surroundings. "I think you could fit this place in a bathroom stall at that church."

Josephine laughed. "No way."

"Trust me. Anyway, I was here in Tucker Springs going to college. My parents were paying for everything, so I was living the dream. Just studying, playing in a band or two, doing some partying. Didn't have to worry about a job or anything." I took a deep breath. Just saying this part never got much easier. "And then I came out to my parents."

Josephine's eyes widened. "What'd they do?"

"They flew in with our pastor and my godparents, and tried to take me back to L.A. They were going to try to force me into one of those programs that makes you straight. You know what I'm talking about?"

She shuddered. "Yeah, I do."

"Well, fortunately, since I was an adult, they couldn't. Didn't stop them from trying, but . . . yeah. And then they completely cut me off. Cut off my tuition, closed my bank account, canceled my credit cards, took my car back, the whole works. I had to get on my own feet almost overnight with no real work experience and absolutely nothing to my name." I paused. "The worst part, though? They told me as long as I was gay, I was no son of theirs, and I haven't heard from them since."

"How long ago was that?"

"It's been . . ." I ran the dates through my head. "Man, it's been years now."

"And you haven't talked to them since?" A note of disappointment crept into her tone. "At all?"

"Nope."

"But you still got on your feet?" Josephine held my gaze now, like she was searching for something in my expression. "I mean, you did okay? Even after they cut you off?"

"Yeah. It was hard for a while. I did a lot of couch-surfing, and believe me, there is no one on the planet who knows more ways to prepare Ramen. But I got it together."

She was quiet for a moment. Then, speaking so softly I almost couldn't hear her, she asked, "Do you miss them?"

"Sometimes. I miss being part of a family, but to be honest? The longer I've been away from them, the more I'm at peace with it."

Josephine swallowed, and she lowered her gaze. "How do you make peace with your family kicking you out?"

"Well, think about it." I kept my tone as gentle as possible. "Would you want to be friends with someone who thinks you're less than human, or that you're not worthy of being loved?"

Her brow furrowed.

"It's kind of like when you break up with someone," I said. "It sucks, and it hurts, and it takes a while to get over it, but then one day you realize that if that's how they are, then you really *are* better off without them in your life. Doesn't make it easy, and it doesn't stop hurting, but it does get better."

Josephine said nothing for a long moment. I wasn't sure if I should keep talking or just let her digest everything, but I also wasn't sure what I could say.

After a while, she said, "So what do you do now? You're just a musician?"

"No, I play in bands for fun. Never really suited me as a professional thing, and I'm not even in a band at the moment. My job is"—I pointed at the sleeve on my left arm—"tattoos."

"Really? So you're an atheist, and you tattoo people for a living while you play in rock bands, but you're . . ." She looked around. "Here?"

"You'd better believe it." I gestured behind us in the direction of the kitchen where all of the other kids had gone. "All these kids are in the same boat you are, and when I was out on my ass a few years ago, I would have given my right arm for a place like this."

"Even in a church?"

"Didn't matter where. I just needed people. You know, someone there who still treated me like I was a human being."

Josephine's shoulders sagged beneath her blouse. She folded her arms and leaned forward, resting them on her legs. "I really miss my family."

"I know you do. Sometimes I still miss mine. But if they think you're not good enough for them, then . . . they're not good enough for you."

"How do you live without a family, though?"

"Family's not all there is. There's friends. I didn't know a soul in Tucker Springs when I came here, but now I've got a bunch of great friends here. In fact, one of my buddies from that church I grew up in moved here a while back, and he's living with one of my best friends." I paused. "And you know, sometimes there are advantages to not having your family around."

"What do you mean?"

I offered a cautious grin. "Well, for one thing, you don't have to spend the holidays with people you don't like."

Josephine laughed, but then her voice cracked, and she clapped a hand over her mouth as her cheeks reddened. "Damn it."

"It's all right. I'm telling you, my friend can help you with that. So, here." I dug an old gas receipt out of my wallet and wrote Diana's phone number on the back of it. "Give her a call, and tell her you know Seth Wheeler. And don't worry about paying for the lessons. She and I will work something out."

She smiled, folding up the receipt and slipping it into her purse. "Thanks. And thanks for talking to me."

"Anytime." I gestured over my shoulder toward the kitchen. "Why don't we go see about getting you something to eat? Sounds like they're going to turn this place into a dodge ball court before too long."

We got up, and when I turned around, Darren was there, staring slack-jawed at me. Josephine wandered past him, and he watched her go, blinking a few times.

"What?" I asked.

"That . . ." He shook his head. "I don't know what you did, but . . ."

"It worked."

"Yes, it did." He held my gaze. "I shouldn't be so surprised you're good with kids, but . . ."

"I just know where she's coming from."

"Well, do feel free to come down here anytime," he said. "These kids could definitely use someone like you."

I smiled. "I'd be happy to."

"Thanks."

By all rights, we should have broken eye contact and headed toward the kitchen. We didn't, though, and now my heart started doing weird things.

I cleared my throat. "You're, um, sure you want an atheist around here all the time?"

"I want *you* around here all the time."

The statement made me jump. It took me a second to realize he meant he wanted me around to help with the outreach. Right?

I forced a grin. "Is this part of that whole 'love thy enemy' thing?"

Darren frowned. "You're not the enemy, Seth."

And still, we kept looking at each other.

My heart pounded. This wasn't the time or place. And Darren? I couldn't. I just—

"Well, I'm not your enemy now," I said. "But we'll see what happens if we're on opposite sides on the dodge ball court."

"Oh, really? I've had more practice than you, you know."

I clapped his shoulder and we started toward the kitchen. "I guess we'll see if it's done you any good. I mean, as long as you're not scared."

"Scared?" Darren raised an eyebrow. "Bring it on."

"I can't believe he nailed me right in the goddamned face." I rubbed the tender spot above my cheekbone.

Darren laughed as he followed me up the stairs to our apartments. "I told you, didn't I?"

"I thought you were kidding."

"I never kid when it comes to dodge ball." He paused. "And I'd like to take this opportunity to sincerely thank you for introducing a few new vocabulary words to my kids."

I didn't even try to appear sheepish as I glanced over my shoulder. "You really think they've never heard anything like that before?"

"I'm sure they have. But probably not echoing through a church sanctuary."

"Okay, fair point."

We stopped in that hallway between our apartments. Immediately, the awkwardness started creeping in. Something about this place, apparently. It always felt like we were hovering in some neutral space, like this hallway was some level of Limbo. There was always that feeling like we were at a crossroads.

Darren cleared his throat. "By the way, I know I mentioned this before, but what you did for Josephine, that was . . . that was really great."

"Yeah, well. I don't know if I did much for her faith. Sorry about that."

"At this point, I don't care." Darren scratched his neck. "I'm supposed to tell her to have faith in Christ, but the way Josephine sees things right now, that faith is the reason she's in this mess. What she needs now is a roof over her head, food in her mouth, and people who won't throw her out on the street." He exhaled and lowered his hand. "So that's the part I'm trying to take care of."

"Looks like she's off to a good start, then. With everything you guys are doing."

"We do our best. And I really do appreciate you going down there tonight. I think you're exactly what those kids need." A faint smile curled the corners of his mouth. "Even if a church isn't your favorite place in the world."

I shrugged. "Well, it's a lot different from the other ones I've been to. And so are . . ." *You. You're the polar opposite of what I know. You shouldn't be. You shouldn't exist.* I rocked back and forth from my heels to the balls of my feet, trying to do something with all this nervous energy. "You're not like other ministers I've known."

"I used to be," he said quietly.

I stopped moving. "Really?"

Darren nodded and leaned against his door frame. "I told you I'm from a family of missionaries. I was a pretty hardcore evangelist when I was younger."

"So, what changed?"

"I spent two years in Africa."

"Missionary work?"

"Yeah, but it wasn't one of those 'go in and convert the natives' things." He shifted a little, shoulder still pressed against the door frame. "I mean, it was, but we were also helping this village get on its feet after one of the civil wars. Putting in some wells and things like that."

"So Peace Corps type work."

"You could call it that." His eyes lost focus. "And it's another world over there, you know? People dying of things we don't even think about anymore." He swallowed, and I thought he might've shuddered. "I'll never forget this kid I met there. By the time he was eight years old, he could handle an AK-47 and he'd helped bury most of his own family, but he'd never tasted clean water."

"Oh man." I swallowed. "I can't even imagine."

"No, you definitely can't unless you've seen it." Darren shuddered. "So anyway, some of the guys I was with, they were talking one night about how blessed we all are. Seeing those third-world conditions made them realize how much God blesses us, and how good God is." His lips tightened for a moment, and he met my eyes. "And the whole time they were talking, all I could think of was that kid. I'm blessed beyond words, but what about him?"

"Wow. That must have been jarring." And probably would have knocked the faith right out of me if I'd still been a believer.

"It was. And it changed me. It really did. I do believe God is good, of course, and I'm certainly blessed, but when I see people in those conditions, I don't think about how good God's made my life compared to that. What I see is all the work we need to do for each other, you know? I'm still moved to share the Gospel with people, but I think I'm more like . . ." He dropped his gaze, and some color bloomed in his cheeks.

"What?"

Darren laughed softly. "I guess a Biblical parable isn't really what you want to hear."

I shrugged. "I don't know. I can see the value in a lot of those stories. Try me."

"Well, you know the Good Samaritan story as well as anyone. And especially after what I saw during my missionary work, I find that someone who's starving, or homeless, or suffering isn't as inclined to listen as someone who has food and a roof. So I guess . . ." He searched my eyes for a moment. "I guess I feel like God's calling me to bandage the people on the side of the road, and let Christ handle the rest."

"That's a . . ." I exhaled. "It's a refreshing switch from what I'm used to, believe me."

And there it was: that eye contact that locked, lingered, and seemed to tug me toward him. I had no idea what to say right then. Nothing that didn't sound awkward, or wouldn't come out as "You almost sound good enough to date, but fuck you for being a

Christian." Because he wasn't the kind of Christian who scared me. He was Darren, and he was amazing, and I was staring at him.

I muffled a cough and tried to find somewhere else to look, at least until I got my bearings about me, but my eyes kept going right back to his.

"This keeps happening," he said, almost whispering.

I swallowed. "What's that?"

"Whenever we're here"—he waved a hand around our narrow confines—"between our apartments, we seem to be inept at just calling it a night."

"Well, given how our evenings have turned out a few times, maybe we're just out of practice. At just walking away."

Darren nodded slowly. "Or maybe it means we shouldn't keep trying to walk away."

The whole world shifted under me. "We . . ."

He pushed himself off the door frame and stepped closer to me, driving my heart rate skyward. "Seth, you and I aren't all that different. We believe different things, but we're just two men. And I think in some ways, we want the same things."

"We want the same things? Like what?"

"You tell me." He leaned toward me, and the warm brush of his fingertips across my five o'clock shadow turned my spine to liquid. His lips touched mine, and I wrapped my arms around him.

"Should you be doing this?" I asked.

"I'm not." His breath warmed the side of my face. "We are."

"You know what I mean."

Darren drew back and met my eyes. "I do, and quite honestly, I can't convince myself there's anything wrong with this."

In that moment, neither could I.

CHAPTER 11

Somewhere in the middle of a kiss, I managed to find my house key in my pocket, and murmured, "We should get inside."

Darren nodded, pulling back a little and licking his lips. "Sooner the better."

Oh, hell. With the hunger in his eyes, I was half-tempted to see how much we could get away with right here between our apartments. But the lube and condoms necessary for what I really wanted were in my bedroom, so with some cursing and trembling, I unlocked my door and let us in.

Halfway down the short hall, I couldn't wait, and turned around, and we segued from walking to kissing like it was the next logical step.

This wasn't the way we'd kissed before. It was different. Slower. Calmer. No one pushed anyone up against anything. Hands were gentle and every motion was languid, mouths moving together like we wanted to savor every taste. We'd always been in such a rush. This time, there was no less urgency, but the need to hurry had cooled, like we didn't have to scramble to get to our destination because we were already there.

Darren's lips left mine, and he whispered, "We're both still sweaty from that dodge ball game. Maybe . . ."

"Maybe we should grab a shower."

"Yes." His lip just grazed mine. "That."

"Good idea." I ran my fingers through his hair. "We'll get there." A light kiss. Another. "In a minute."

Darren didn't seem to mind. He pulled me closer, his fingers pressing into my skin through my clothes, and my knees shook as I yielded to a kiss that was getting progressively more demanding.

"Fuck." I gasped for air. "Okay. About that shower." I dragged him back a step toward the bathroom. "We should get on that. Like now."

He laughed. "Good idea."

In the shower, we got as far as getting soap on our hands, and then we were back in each other's arms. Slippery hands ran over wet skin. Our bodies were slick, hot, pressed together under the water while we made out like we had all night to turn each other on.

Then Darren faced the water. As he did, the sharp black lines and letters between his shoulder blades jolted something deep in my gut. Immediately, the other night's worries tried to come crashing back in, but I wasn't letting them ruin this moment. Regrets and reservations could wait until tomorrow morning. Tonight, Darren was mine.

I wrapped my arms around him and pressed my lips to the side of his neck. "My God, I want you so bad."

Darren moaned and rubbed his ass against my cock, his skin slick and hot from soap and water. I could barely think, overwhelmed by this slow pantomime, this parody of everything I needed to do to him. I wanted to be touching him just like this, our bodies this close together, but I wanted to be deep inside him too. Damn the need for lube and rubbers, because I would have sold my soul to be able to just fuck him. Right here, right now.

"You want me to fuck you, don't you?" I growled in his ear.

Darren whimpered and pressed back against me.

I kissed just below his jaw. "Don't you?"

"Yes. We should . . . bedroom."

"Mmm, I like that idea." I slid a hand over his hip and deliberately brushed his cock with my fingertips. "Except I like this too."

He moaned, wriggling against me. "Seth . . ."

"Hmm?"

"Bedroom."

The forcefulness of that one word almost made me come. I exhaled against his neck, then kissed it and whispered, "Let's go."

We quickly rinsed off, then toweled off—sort of—and hurried into my bedroom.

Now that was the kiss I recognized: breathless, groping, demanding. Fingers raked through wet hair. His hard cock ground against mine. I cursed between kisses, and now and then I was sure he did the same, and then we tumbled into bed and—

"Wait!" He arched off the bed and grimaced.

"What? What's wrong?"

He winced. "Tattoo's still a little itchy."

"Shit. Sorry."

"Don't worry about it. Just means I—" he caught me off guard and flipped me onto my back and straddled me "—get to be on top."

All the air left my lungs at once. "You won't . . . you won't hear me objecting."

"Excellent." He leaned down and kissed me quickly. "Condoms?"

Oh God. I so love it when you take charge.

Moistening my lips, I gestured at the nightstand. He pulled the necessities from the drawer. Thank fuck I'd left a few condoms and a half-empty bottle of lube over here that first night, because there just wasn't time to go get them from Darren's apartment.

As he rolled the condom onto my cock, I said, "You do like being in charge, don't you?"

He grinned down at me. "I think you like me being in charge."

I licked my lips again. "I'm not going to argue with that."

"Didn't think you would." He poured some lube onto his hand. Neither of us said anything. This close to fucking him, I was too turned on for banter. Hell, for speech at all.

Darren put the lube bottle aside, and my whole body tingled with anticipation as he lifted his hips. I steadied my cock with one hand, his hip with the other, and we both held our breath as he lowered himself onto me. I closed my eyes, digging my teeth into my lower lip as he took me a little at a time. Holy fuck, he felt amazing. The tight, slick, up-and-down motion drove me right out of my damned mind.

I reached up to pull him down to me, but he grabbed my wrists and pinned them to the bed. I knew he liked to take charge, but it still caught me by surprise. And turned me on beyond belief. Curling my hands into useless fists, I pressed my heels into the bed and thrust upward, complementing his rhythm and forcing myself deeper inside him.

He leaned over me, but stayed just out of reach of my lips, holding my gaze but denying me a kiss. I was completely pinned. Completely at his mercy.

"I've been dying for this," he whispered. "Every time I see you, I . . ." He trailed off into a soft moan.

I managed to get one hand free, and reached between us to stroke him. He gasped, throwing his head back and riding me a little faster.

"Like that?" I asked.

"Oh, yeah."

Our eyes locked just like they always did. We held each other's gazes, barely blinking, and even when my eyes tried to tear up, I couldn't look anywhere but right at him. Just watching him, seeing his skin flush and the cords stand out from his neck as he picked up speed, made me almost as crazy as fucking him, and every thrust sent me closer to coming as much from the sight of him as the slick, hot motion of my cock moving in and out of him.

Darren screwed his eyes shut. His cock stiffened in my hand. I stroked faster. He rode me harder, and as he came, his semen coated my palm, making my strokes slippery and hot, and I lost it. I swore, and groaned, and thrust upward to get as far into him as I could get, and we both shuddered and fucking shattered.

His hips stopped. My hand stopped. Darren shuddered one last time. As he sank down to me, I wrapped my arms around him and found his lips with mine. We were both panting. Both shaking. Both sweaty, unsteady, and breathing too hard to kiss, but we did it anyway.

He broke away. "That was hot."

"Yes, it was," I whispered. I very nearly added, *It's always hot when we're together*, but didn't dare.

So I just kissed him again.

The silence that followed sex with Darren always got awkward in a hurry, so we didn't give the awkwardness a chance to set in. As soon as we'd calmed down enough to kiss without passing out, we made out until we were both turned on again. After a second go-around, we took another shower, which led to a third time, which exhausted the fuck out of both of us. After that, we slept.

Which saved the awkwardness until the morning after.

Half-dressed and barefoot, we clung to our coffee cups. The kitchens in these apartments were damned small, and we had both backed ourselves up against opposite counters as if we could push the cabinets apart and create a few extra inches between us.

Same shit, different morning. I had no idea what to say. Restlessness had me shifting my weight, trying to get rid of some energy that refused to be satisfied by anything less than running like hell out of this room.

Except we were in my apartment this time. There was no quick, polite exit that wouldn't make me sound like a complete asshole.

Darren rinsed his empty coffee cup and set it in the sink. "I should probably get going."

"I guess I should get my day started too," I said. "Have to go do some work in the shop before I open."

"No rest for the weary, am I right?"

I laughed, and he flashed a quick grin that did all kinds of screwy shit to my balance and blood pressure. Then he left the room, leaving me to my heartbeat and spinning head as he went into my bedroom to, I guessed, get the rest of his clothes.

I rubbed my temples with my fingers. God, I had no idea what to do. It was a crime against humanity that sex that hot—was Darren even capable of being "meh" in bed?—had to have this kind of weight attached to it.

Something had to give, though. We couldn't keep playing this game.

His footsteps sent my heartbeat ratcheting up again. Funny how the same man could make my blood pressure rise from arousal or from nerves, depending on the time of day and how recently we'd fucked.

He returned to the kitchen, dressed and ready to go, and we walked in silence to my front door. He reached for the doorknob, but hesitated. Time for the awkward small talk, yes?

"I'll, um . . ." He paused, dropping his gaze.

The air between us pulsed with something unspoken. I didn't dare ask what was on his mind. I was too afraid to hear it.

"Seth." He looked me straight in the eye. "We need to talk."

My stomach flipped. "Okay. Let's, um, let's talk."

Hooking his thumbs in the pockets of his jeans, he leaned against the door. "What exactly are we doing?"

Fuck. Here we go.

"Um, well . . ." I reached up to scratch the back of my neck. "I'm not sure, to be honest."

"Neither am I." He shifted his weight. Then did it again. "Listen, I'm not after a long-term commitment or anything. Don't get me wrong. But I'm not going to keep doing this yo-yo thing. We can't keep our hands off each other, and then we sleep together, and then it's awkward, and . . ." He exhaled hard. "And we just keep going back and forth from 'just friends' and neighbors to dragging each other into bed."

I couldn't face him. Speaking was out of the question.

"I'm not going to keep playing this game and just having a string of one-night stands together." He paused for a few long seconds. "I won't push you into something you don't want, but quite honestly, I don't believe you when you say you don't want it."

I managed a quiet, nervous laugh. "Didn't you once say something about not being the aggressive type?"

"With most people, I'm not. But I told you it's different when I see something *I* want."

Glancing at him, I gulped.

He inched closer, and his tone softened. "Why do we keep fighting this so hard?"

"I . . ." *Can't be with someone like you no matter how much I want you?* "I told you. I'm not in a good place for a relationship."

"Okay. I can accept that. But . . ." He held my gaze so intently it was unnerving. "Where does that leave us? I mean, are we friends? Is this"—he gestured down the hall toward my bedroom—"something you want to keep doing?"

I chewed the inside of my cheek. "I guess that depends on whether or not it'll make things weird." *Or if it's already made them weird.* "Or if it's something you aren't comfortable with. The casual sexual thing."

"I'm not sure how I feel about it, to be honest. It's never something I saw myself doing. Whatever this is, it . . . I guess it just happened, and there's only so many times it can keep happening before I have to figure that out. If I'm comfortable continuing like this, I mean, or if I want us to take things seriously."

I didn't know what to say to that.

"And to be perfectly blunt," he said, "whenever I do think about that, I just can't help thinking whether we continue this casually or more seriously, we're going to end up in the same place."

My heart jumped into my throat. "And that place is, where?"

"Only one way to find out." His eyes locked on mine, and my stomach somersaulted, especially when he added, "Personally, I'd like to skip the games and take the direct route."

But does all of this terrify you like it does me?

"Listen, the truth is . . ." I paused, chewing my lip.

Darren's fingers tapped against the door, a gesture that I hoped came from restlessness and not impatience. "The truth is, what?"

"Not something you're going to want to hear."

"Try me."

I rubbed some stiffness out of the back of my neck. "As much as we get along, and as much as we *rock* in bed together, I really don't think we're cut out to be in a relationship."

"Oh." He was quiet for a moment. "Why?"

"Well." *Here goes. No turning back.* "It's . . . I'll be honest. It has to do with our beliefs."

"What do you mean? The fact that you're an atheist and I'm a Christian?"

"And that you're a minister."

"What does that have to do with anything?" He wasn't hostile. Not even a little put off, from the sound of it. Which only made this that much harder, and set my teeth on edge. *Damn you for being so fucking easygoing!*

"I told you I was raised in a fundamentalist household, and I was disowned by my family and excommunicated from my church. And I—"

"And I don't condone what they did," he said. "You should know me well enough by now to know something like that would horrify me."

"Maybe so, but it was their beliefs that led them to do what they did."

Darren shifted his weight. "So, if you took my beliefs out of the equation, would we be having this conversation? Is that the only thing keeping you from seeing if we can make this work?"

"It's not exactly a small thing."

"No, it isn't." He narrowed his eyes. "But it's one of those things we could work around *if* we thought it was worth it."

"I never said it wouldn't be worth it," I snapped. "But some obstacles just can't—"

"Obstacles?" He forced out a breath. "So what if we have a difference in beliefs? Do you think everyone who's ever dated has been in one hundred percent agreement on everything?"

"Of course not. But there are things that are difficult to compromise on. And it's not just what you believe. Correct me if I'm wrong, but aren't you supposed to help people get saved? Evangelize? *Convert?*"

His expression hardened. "I'm not interested in converting you."

"Yeah? And how long will that last?" I asked through clenched teeth. "Seriously, how long can you really see yourself being with me when I'm—"

"If I couldn't see myself with you as you are right now," he said, his voice unsteady, "I wouldn't have started this conversation."

My heart plummeted into my feet. "I just don't see how we could make this work. How I could ever relax into our relationship without waiting for the other shoe to drop."

Darren blinked. "The other shoe to drop? What do you mean?"

"I mean, I don't know how to *not* be afraid of what happened with my family."

"You mean . . ." He moistened his lips. "You mean, you're afraid I'd do to you what your family did? Even though I'm gay too?"

"I know it doesn't make sense. Not rationally. But the fact is, you're a Christian. My life was turned on its ass by Christians because of their beliefs. And . . ." I paused, struggling to find the words. "You're like two sides of a coin for me. You're the man I can't stop thinking about and couldn't stop wanting if I tried. But you're also the man my family wishes I was, and would take me back if I was. You're too much of *them.*"

The words hit harder than I thought they would. And farther below the belt. And only after they were out, and after Darren's eyes had widened in *Did I just hear what I think I just heard?* fashion, did I realize what I'd actually said.

Then his eyes narrowed again. "So your family and your church booted you out because you're gay." The tense undercurrent in his voice made my heart stop. Laid-back Darren at the end of his tether.

"So you can't get involved with me, another gay man, solely because I belong to the same religion they do? Even though every time we've even discussed our beliefs, I've been just as civil and open-minded as you have? You know, *not* beating you over the head and proselytizing like they apparently did?"

I opened my mouth to speak, but what to say? I'd wanted him to finally react to something, to quit being so calm and perfect and unruffled by *everything*, and now he was coming unraveled faster than I could cope with. Faster than I could adapt to.

I swallowed. "You don't think—"

"You know, I can't win." He threw up his hands. "There are Christians who openly and rather vehemently shun me because I'm gay. And then in the gay community, I'm kept at arm's length because I'm a Christian. No matter which group I'm around, I'm shut out for being one of 'them.'" And all at once, the anger crumbled in favor of something a lot less hostile and a lot more painful. His voice wavered just slightly as he said, "Do you really think I would ever use my faith as a weapon against you, Seth?"

I flinched. "Do you think I thought my own family would?"

"You want to put me in the same category as Westboro Baptist while you're at it?" The anger was back in full force, but the waver remained, like he was as close to losing his temper as he was to just breaking down. "How is what you're saying to me any different from what everyone has done to you? Because of a vital part of who I am, a part of me I have never *once* tried to force on you or even bring into a conversation more than I thought you were comfortable with, you can't be around me?"

"I never said I couldn't be around you. I just don't see how we could make a relationship work."

He snorted. "Yeah. No kidding. When you can't see me as anything other than 'one of them'"—he added emphatic air quotes—"just like your family can't see you as anything other than a gay man." He shook his head and released a sharp breath. "You know, you're so worried I'm going to hammer my beliefs down your throat, or try to convert you every chance I get, but do you even listen to yourself, Seth? You brought our beliefs into this, not me."

I folded my arms tightly across my chest. "What do you want me to do?"

"I want you to stop equating me with the people who hurt you. *I've* never hurt you. Just because I'm a believer does not mean—"

"You're not just a believer, Darren, you're a minister. You live, breathe, and preach the beliefs that damn near ruined my fucking life."

"No. No, I do not." He stabbed a finger at me. "I had no part in that, Seth. What I live and breathe is the set of beliefs that makes me want to help kids off the street after they've been thrown out by parents like yours. How can you put me in the same category as your family?"

"Because you're fucking preaching out of the same goddamned book they used to fucking disown me!"

Darren stared at me, his eyes wide and lips apart.

"Sorry." I paused, shaking my head. "I'm—I'm sorry. I didn't mean to curse, I . . ."

His eyebrows rose. "You think the cursing was the most offensive part of that?"

"Darren—"

"No." He put up a hand. "I've heard enough." He reached for the doorknob. "And I'm glad we had this talk now. The sooner the truth came out, the better."

There was a two-second window between his hand landing on the doorknob and him making his escape. A few more seconds for him to get across the hall into his own apartment. Maybe fifteen total, a short window during which I could have stopped him. Or at least tried to stop him.

But I didn't.

I let him go.

My door slammed.

Seconds later, so did his.

I dropped onto the sofa and sighed, rubbing my forehead with the heels of my hands. I didn't even know what to feel. Guilty? Relieved? Both? Fuck, I had no idea. All I knew was Darren was gone.

Right across the hall, but definitely gone.

CHAPTER 12

I made it through the next day on autopilot. The day after that, I could barely concentrate on my work, so I canceled all my afternoon and evening appointments, as well as the next day's. That would hurt come the first of the month, but I'd have an easier time sorting out a late rent payment with Al than I would fixing or explaining a botched tattoo.

This never happened to me. I'd worked on a giant, elaborate back piece just hours after a massive fight ended my last relationship. I didn't let shit distract me from my work, but now, I was lucky I knew which way to point the tattoo needle. What the hell?

I couldn't stop thinking about Darren. It was like two film reels playing in my head at the same time. One was a montage of everything that made me miss him: the outreach, talking over beers, having amazing sex. And the other, running right beside the first, was that argument. I simultaneously saw us laughing over a shared joint and Darren looking at me like he was *this close* to tears. I heard him coming in the same instant I heard the door slamming.

I was losing my motherfucking mind.

Finally, I gave up on trying to clear my mind and decided I needed to cloud it a bit. I grabbed my jacket, the one with the plastic bag in the pocket, and went up to the roof. I pulled a chair and the small table out from under the tarp, and put them in my usual spot against the railing.

I put the bag and lighter on the table, the mint tin clinking quietly on the hard plastic surface, but I didn't roll the joint yet. There wasn't much in the world I wanted more than to get as stoned as I possibly could tonight. Alcohol would only depress me. The weed would let me check out and not give a fuck for a few hours.

Except my head was already a muddled mess. Too restless to get stoned? Wasn't that an oxymoron? But, hell, I was so distracted and wound up, I couldn't even remember the steps that would get me from this point to blissfully baked off my ass.

I couldn't sit still, so I finally got up and paced back and forth beside the railing. The wind fluttered the edges of the plastic bag still sitting on the table, but my lighter and the mint tin kept it from flying away.

I glanced at the door leading to the stairs. A memory flickered through my mind of Darren wandering up here, sitting down, and joining me for a smoke. Sitting in one of those chairs across from that plastic table and taking a drag like he'd done this before. Totally relaxed and friendly, no clue at all about the conversation we'd eventually have in my living room.

We'd just been two guys that night. We'd smoked enough to relax, but we'd still been coherent enough to talk. For a while, he hadn't been a minister, and I had never been hurt enough by my church and family to be gun-shy about him anyway. Just two guys, a couple of joints, and an hour or two of talking like we'd been friends all our lives.

Just like we had when we'd talked over beers the first night. And when I'd tattooed his back. And while we'd been out hiking together. And after the night we'd gone to the outreach.

Exactly how I'd always imagined it would be with the perfect boyfriend.

All the restless energy evaporated, and I sank into the chair, letting my face fall into my hands. How long had I spent psyching myself up to end things with him before they'd really even started? Trying to work up the nerve to find the words to explain why, no matter how much I wanted him, I couldn't be with him?

But this wasn't the right ending. This was never what I'd wanted.

Seth, your parents cost you a lot of good things in your life. Michael's words echoed in the back of my mind. *Don't let them cost you this too.*

Oh God. What had I done?

And what the hell did I do now?

Twenty minutes later, at the front door of Lights Out, the bouncer gave me a quick nod and waved me in.

"Jason's in his office," he shouted, and I thanked him over the music before heading upstairs.

As usual, Jason was swimming in paperwork, his shoulder tight and probably painful as fuck by now, but he relaxed a little when I stepped into his office.

"Hey," he said. "What's up?"

"Want to take a break?" I asked. "I'm guessing you could use it."

He eyed me, and I suspected my own tension was written all over me as much as him. He pushed his chair back and rose. Neither of us spoke as we left his office and headed down the hall. Our feet clanged on the metal stairwell up to the roof where his employees took their breaks when it was nice out, and where he and I sometimes hung out when I came by to visit. I may as well have been a damned cat for all the time I spent on roofs these days.

Jason rolled his shoulders and reached up to rub the side of his neck.

"Man, you ever going to dump some of that crap on someone else?" I asked. "Before this place kills you?"

Jason lowered his hand, rolled his shoulder one more time, and then smiled. "Actually, now that the cash flow's improving, I'm working on hiring someone. Got a few interviews this week, so with any luck? Within two weeks, yes, I'll be dumping this crap on someone else."

"About fucking time," I said.

"Tell me about it." He folded his arms and rested them on the concrete railing. "So what's up? You look like you haven't slept in a week."

"Pretty close." I rubbed my own stiffening neck. "You remember my neighbor? The minister?"

"The one you're fucking?"

"*Was* fucking."

"Oh."

I closed my eyes. Rubbed my forehead with the heel of my hand. "You ever done something that made perfect sense at the time, and then after the fact, you realized it was a colossal fuck-up?"

"You mean like buying a house with my ex?" he muttered.

"Exactly." I blew out a breath.

"So what happened?"

"I broke it off with him because . . . because after everything I went through when I was younger, I don't trust religious people."

Jason nodded. "So you broke it off with this guy because he's a Christian?"

Heat rushed into my cheeks, and I avoided Jason's eyes. "It made perfect sense until right about the time he was walking out of my apartment. I thought I was doing the right thing by nipping it in the bud, but right then, I realized I'd made a huge goddamned mistake. And now . . ." I ran a hand through my hair. "I have no idea what to do."

"Talk to him?" Jason said. "See if you can try again?"

"Assuming he'll talk to me." I rested my hip against the concrete railing. "I mean, I'm not sure we can make it work anyway, but we—"

"Who says you can't make it work? Just because he's a minister?"

The Seth from a few days ago wanted to lash out and scoff. *Just because he's a minister? That's a pretty significant thing when I've been fucked over by people who buy what he's selling.*

But it was amazing how insignificant something like that became when the alternative was missing out on someone like Darren.

I shook my head. "I thought we couldn't. Maybe we can't. I mean, think about it. How can we make something like this work? Religious beliefs aren't something people can compromise on. It's like having kids: there's no halfway. But I . . . Fuck, I don't even know anymore. I've been guarding myself from religious people for so long after what happened with my parents and this just came out of nowhere."

"This being what happened with your neighbor?" Jason arched an eyebrow. "Or this being you finding someone you can see yourself with, and then pushing him away because you're scared? And I don't mean scared of what he believes, but of what he *is*."

"Meaning?"

"Meaning I've known you for a long time, and I've seen you shy away from one guy after another for all kinds of reasons when the real reason was totally transparent, but I never said anything because I've never seen you get this hung up on a guy before."

I shifted my weight, my sneaker scuffing on the concrete. "Is that right?"

Jason nodded. "The only reason I'm saying something now is that just listening to you, I can tell you think just like I do that you're fucking up something you shouldn't."

I wasn't sure I was ready to hear the answer, but I asked anyway: "So what's the real reason, then?"

He didn't reply immediately, and I thought he might be waiting for me to put the pieces together myself. Finally, he said, "I know you have legitimate reasons to be wary of people of the religious persuasion. I'm not discounting that here. But what happens if you take religion completely out of the picture?"

Eyeing Jason, I said, "It's kind of a moot point because his religion is a rather huge part of his life, don't you think?"

"So if he walked up here right now and told you he'd renounced his beliefs, become a card-carrying atheist, and never wanted to set foot in a church again as long as he lived, you'd jump into a relationship with him without thinking twice? No fear?"

I swallowed.

"That's what I thought. And really, wouldn't someone with polar opposite beliefs be the perfect match for you?" He grinned. "You'd always have something to talk about."

Somehow, I managed to laugh. "Okay, I can't argue with that."

"Exactly." He paused for a long moment. "The thing is, I don't think it's his beliefs that are really bothering you. I mean, regardless of why, your family hurt you. You've had *one* solid relationship since then, with a guy who also worked you over—which had nothing to do with religion—and that was four years ago. No guy has been able to get near you since then."

I stared out at the dark shadows of the distant mountains. My neck prickled and blood pounded in my ears as the uncomfortable truth set in.

"Face it," he said softly. "You're terrified of getting hurt. It's not the fact that this guy might have something in common with your parents that's scaring you. That's just a convenient excuse to hide behind so you don't have to face the truth."

"Which is?"

"That if this guy walked away from you, for any reason, it might hurt as bad as when your family turned you away." He put a hand on my shoulder and squeezed gently. "You're not afraid of Christians, Seth. You're afraid of being loved."

The words hit me in the gut. I closed my eyes. I wanted to get defensive and tell him he was full of shit, that he had no idea what he was talking about, but I couldn't.

"I know this isn't easy for you." Jason squeezed my shoulder again. "But I think letting this guy go is a huge mistake. You need to make things right with him. Even if things don't work out in the long run, I get the feeling this isn't how you think it should end."

I sighed. "At this point, though, I'm not even sure what I can do. I told him where I was coming from—where I thought I was coming from—and it . . . it didn't go well."

"Letting it fester isn't going to fix it."

"Do you think anything will?"

"Well, I think your best bet is to quit being a stubborn idiot, and go talk to him."

I said nothing.

"Maybe you guys can make it work," Jason said, his tone gentler now. "Maybe you can't. But I know you: you're the kind of guy who will move on if things don't work out, but if you walk away without even giving it a go, you *will* regret it until the day you die."

I couldn't look at him. He was right, of course.

"I think I hurt him pretty badly, though."

"Just talk to him. Hopefully he'll listen."

Yeah. Hopefully.

But I couldn't bring myself to bank on it.

CHAPTER 13

Tonight. We were going to discuss this tonight. My conversation with Jason had been banging around inside my head for a couple of days now, and if I was ever going to sleep again, Darren and I needed to talk. Tonight, damn it.

Assuming he didn't tell me off or blow me off. Sitting in my living room waiting for him to get home, I caught myself wishing I believed in some higher power I could pray to just to beg for Darren to hear me out. There was something ironic about that. And maybe I'd have appreciated that irony if I wasn't wound so tight and trying not to get sick with nerves.

If he thought I was an asshole, he had every right. If he refused to discuss anything with me, I couldn't blame him. That didn't stop me from hoping and hoping he didn't walk away.

The quiet creak of stairs under feet sent my heart rate skyrocketing. *Now or never, before I lose my nerve.*

I opened the door as he was unlocking his.

"Darren."

He froze, but still didn't turn around.

"Listen, um." I cleared my throat. "Can we talk?"

He took his key out of the lock and slid it into his pocket. For a moment, he didn't move, and I thought he might push open the door and go into his apartment. But then he slowly turned around, and I braced myself for icy eyes and tight lips.

As we faced each other across the dim hallway, though, I would have given anything for icy eyes and tight lips. Cold indifference or even barely contained fury would have been so much easier to swallow than the palpable hurt in his eyes. Like it was painful for him to even be in my presence.

"Do you want to come in?" I asked.

He didn't move. "Let's try talking first. Then we'll see how it goes."

"You want to do this out here?"

"Unless you think anyone's going to join us."

I couldn't tell if that was supposed to be sarcastic, or if there was an underlying plea of *let's just do this now before I have to walk away.*

I opened my mouth to speak, but he beat me to the punch: "On second thought, maybe it *would* be easier if we were sitting down."

"You sure?"

He nodded.

We moved into my apartment and sat in my living room. I took the recliner, and he took the middle of the couch. And no matter how much I wanted to, I couldn't make myself face him.

Stanley wandered in, gave each of us a look of disdain, and then trotted out of the room. Raised voices terrified him, and even the tension before an argument was enough to send him scurrying under my bed. I watched him go, grimacing as more guilt piled on. Even my cat was upset? Way to go, Seth.

Finally, Darren broke the silence.

"This is about the other morning, isn't it?" His tone betrayed nothing.

Without turning to him, I nodded. "I wanted to apologize."

"But I can't imagine you've changed your mind." Still no emotion either way. "About me."

I chewed my lip. "That's the other thing I wanted to talk to you about."

"Oh. Okay . . ."

"I know we haven't known each other all that long. But things just . . . clicked between us. More than they have for me with any other guy."

"Yeah, I know what you mean," he whispered.

"And I can't lie, I've been edgy ever since you told me you were a minister. But ever since the other day, I've been a wreck."

Darren didn't speak.

I stared at the floor between us. "I know I was too quick to judge you. And I'm sorry for that. I really am."

"I can accept that," he said softly.

I exhaled, some—but not nearly all—of the tension leaving my shoulders. "The thing is, I . . ." Oh, fuck it. Might as well just say it instead of beating around the bush. "Religious differences may seem like a petty thing to avoid, but I've already lost too many people I love over this. I don't . . ." The words stuck in my throat. They were all the wrong words anyway. Fuck, I couldn't get my thoughts straight. Why the hell couldn't I—

"Seth. Look at me."

I hesitated before finally raising my gaze. Speaking was hard enough, but now . . . fuck.

He inclined his head. "You don't, what?"

"What you are, what I am . . . I'm scared of what that'll mean in the future. Because of my past. But even without our differences in beliefs, or my history, I don't . . ." I moistened my lips, and somehow, as I held his gaze, I formed the words: "I'm scared to death of what it would be like to fall for you and then lose you."

Darren's lips parted.

I went on. "But I also don't want to know what it's like to go through life wondering what it might have been like to fall for you. And I'm not sure which risk is more terrifying, to be honest."

He swallowed. "I thought . . . I didn't think you felt that way."

"I'm not sure how I feel," I whispered, because that inexplicably seemed like the only way to keep my voice from shaking. "Just that it hasn't felt like a one-night stand since the beginning, and staying scares me as much as walking away."

His expression hardened again. "So all of that crap about our differences in beliefs, what was that? A smoke screen?"

"It's still . . ." I paused, trying to word this carefully. "It's still something I'm not completely sure how to deal with. I'm not going to lie. But I think what I said and what I was afraid of—what I *thought* I was afraid of—might have been some misdirected self-preservation."

Darren's brow furrowed.

I hesitated, giving myself a chance to collect my thoughts. "As a friend pointed out while he was smacking me over the head with what an idiot I've been, someone with different beliefs is a perfect match for me." Holding eye contact with Darren was difficult, but I made myself do it. "You have as much conviction about your beliefs as I do about mine. You're willing to debate it and discuss it, and even though we disagree, you've never once made me feel inferior or like there's something wrong with me." I lowered my gaze to my hands in my lap. "Not even when I made you feel that way."

"Most of the time you didn't," he said, almost whispering. "That was one of the things I liked about you. We could talk from opposite ends of the spectrum, and still respect each other even if we didn't see eye to eye."

"I do respect you, Darren. And what you believe." I lifted my gaze again. "I'm sorry. I freaked out, and I hurt you. It wasn't what you believed, it was my own hang-ups that threw everything off the rails."

"Well, my reaction . . ." He slowly ran his tongue across his lips. "There's something I should probably tell you. It might explain why I was so upset about what you said."

I sat up a little, steeling myself. "Okay . . ."

His Adam's apple jumped. "I know you're guarded because of what your parents did to you. And no one can blame you for that." He swallowed hard. "But you're not the only one who's been hurt."

My heart dropped.

"I think you need to . . ." Darren laced his fingers together in his lap and focused on them, furrowing his brow like they required deep concentration. "I think you need to understand why I came here. To Tucker Springs." Darren finally raised his head and met my eyes. "Why I had to leave Tulsa."

Something twisted below my ribs. "Go on."

"I was the youth pastor for a church there for four years, and from the start, I figured it would be best to be on the up-and-up about my sexuality. I was dating someone at the time, and I didn't want to have to hide him, or worry about blindsiding anyone."

"People didn't like that?"

Darren shrugged. "Some wigged out. Some didn't care. And yeah, it annoyed me when they decided the youth group was large enough that I really should have an 'assistant youth pastor.' You know, the 'assistant youth pastor' who came to everything where I was with the kids."

"A babysitter?"

"Basically. But she was good with the kids, and she was great to work with, so whatever. I made the best of it." Then Darren took a deep breath, and as he let it out, he set his shoulders back like he was steeling himself against something. "We had four gay kids in the youth group. Four who were out, anyway. And I wondered about a couple of the others, but . . . definitely four. Anyway, that made people even more uncomfortable. Because somehow having them in a group led by a gay man was more dangerous than the teenage girls in the group led by the straight guy who was the youth pastor before me." He rolled his eyes.

"Sounds familiar," I muttered.

Darren shifted uncomfortably. "So, all the kids in the youth group had my email and my cell phone. They knew in no uncertain terms they could contact me, night or day, if they needed anything. Sometimes they called. Frustrated about something they couldn't talk to their parents about, or just having a rough day." He met my eyes. "You know what it's like being a teenager."

I nodded. "Wouldn't go back to those days for anything."

"Hear, hear." He swallowed. "So one night, this kid calls. Chad. He wasn't quite seventeen, and he was one of the four."

"One of the gay kids?"

"Yeah. And he was a mess. Drunk out of his mind, crying, saying he wanted to kill himself."

"Oh my God . . ."

Darren moistened his lips, and his eyes lost focus. "I picked him up at this diner where all the kids like to hang out. He refused to get into the car until I promised not to take him back to his parents' place, so I took him back to mine so he could sober up."

I winced. "Why can I already see where this is going?"

"Because this story always ends the same way," he said bitterly. "When I'd finally convinced him to let me take him home, his parents flipped out, and . . ." He made a *you do the math* gesture.

"Jesus."

"And this poor kid. He was so raw, and in such a bad place, and . . ." Darren whistled and shook his head. "Man, he still refused to let anyone bully him into making an accusation. I was scared to death for him through the whole thing." He paused, clearing his throat. "Every time my phone rang, I was sure someone was going to tell me he'd hurt himself. He just . . . he didn't need that, you know?"

My skin prickled with sick déjà vu. I knew damn well what that kid felt like, and I hadn't had someone like Darren to fall back on. I couldn't begin to imagine what it would be like to have that support, and then have it yanked out from under me.

"So what happened?" I asked.

"The police investigated it. The kid and I both passed polygraphs, and eventually all the charges were dropped." Darren rubbed his forehead, grimacing like this whole train of thought gave him a headache. Maybe it did. "But the congregation still wasn't happy. And the elders, the deaconess, the pastor . . ." He shook his head and sat back, focusing on something across the room. "They had a meeting about it. About me, really."

"That doesn't sound good."

"Not really, no." Darren's lips thinned into a bleached line, and he was quiet for a moment. "When all was said and done, they came to an agreement that it would be better for everyone involved if I left the congregation."

"You're kidding."

"I wish. I mean, I'll go to my grave and still not understand it. What was I supposed to have done, you know?" He ran a hand through his hair. "Just leave him at that diner? Drunk? Tell him he needed to talk to someone else because people might get the wrong idea? As fragile as he—" Darren's voice cracked, and he quickly cleared his throat. "The whole thing was so fucked up."

My heart skipped. I couldn't say what startled me more: the fact that he'd cursed, or how badly his voice had shaken when he did.

Or, as he turned toward me, the extra shine in his eyes.

"I never did a damned thing to any of those kids," he whispered. "But I was kicked out because people got it into their heads that I *might*. Because I'm gay, and so . . ." He waved a hand, and then swiped at his eyes. "Damn it, I'm sorry."

All the air rushed out of my lungs. "And I did the same thing, didn't I?"

Darren said nothing. He didn't move. Didn't look at me.

Heart pounding, I got up and moved to the couch beside him. When I touched his arm, he didn't recoil, so I put my other arm around his shoulders.

"I'm so sorry, Darren," I whispered.

Releasing his breath, he leaned against me, and I wrapped my arms around him.

After a long, silent moment, I asked, "Why was Chad upset that night?"

"What?" Darren's eyes were clearer, but his brow furrowed with confusion.

"The kid you were helping that night." I swallowed. "What . . . what had happened?"

Darren shifted his gaze back down to his hands. "To tell you the truth, I never did get out of him exactly what set him off that night. There was so *much* weighing on him. He'd been really stressed for a while. I was worried about him, and we'd had a few conversations about it. I know he'd just broken up with someone. He felt like an outcast. His parents were putting pressure on him academically and spiritually. To this day, I don't know what the last straw was." Darren sighed. "I think it just boiled down to being a gay teenager with ultraconservative parents in the Midwest."

"Poor kid," I said.

"Yeah, no kidding. And all of that, what I just told you, that's why my brother had such an attitude the day we came to check out the apartment. He's even angrier about what happened to me than I am, and he's terrified it'll happen here too."

"Do you think it will?"

"I don't know." Darren absently brushed a few unruly strands of hair off his forehead. "The congregation is very open-minded, and probably better than half are gay themselves. Plus the pastor's brother was gay. But . . . pastors move around, congregations change. Anything's possible, really."

"Hopefully it'll stay the way it is, then."

"Hopefully." He swallowed hard. "By the way, about that first night . . ." He trailed off, and I didn't say anything as he apparently struggled to find the words. Finally, "I don't usually do that. In fact, I've never done it. Never when I just met a guy. But there was something about you from the beginning that I couldn't ignore. And it was more than the attraction. In a way, knowing you were an atheist made you . . . safer."

"Safer?"

He nodded, avoiding my eyes. "I was pretty sure you were gay, and judging by the bumper sticker, you were an atheist. Which meant I didn't have to be on guard, worried you were going to shove me away because I'm gay. You didn't strike me as the type who'd invite me to a neighborhood barbecue but then subtly try to keep me away from all the kids."

My jaw dropped. "People did that?"

"All the time." He rubbed the back of his neck and sighed. "And after feeling like a pariah for so long, to the point I had to leave the state, I can't even tell you what a relief it was to be having a couple of beers with someone who just took me as I was. And I guess I got more carried away with that—with you—than I usually would." He met my eyes. "Because for the first time in a long time, I felt . . . safe. *You* were safe."

More than anything, that part hit me in the gut. "My God, I am so sorry."

"You couldn't have known what I was dealing with," he said softly.

"But apparently we both know what it's like to be burned for who we are. Maybe we have more common ground than I thought."

"Maybe." Darren held my gaze. "My beliefs aren't going to change. And I don't want yours to change either. You're not a project for me, Seth. I didn't look at you in the beginning and think, 'This guy's great except for one or two things that I'll fix later.'" He paused. "But if we're going to take this forward, then that has to go both ways."

I slipped my hand into his. "I wouldn't try to change you, either. I don't want anything about you to change. Honestly, I don't. I was just . . ."

"Scared?"

"Yeah." I ran my thumb back and forth along his hand. "I am so sorry, Darren."

"You were trying to protect yourself." He squeezed my hand. "I can't really hold that against you." He put his other hand on top of ours. "All I can ask you to do is have faith in me."

I swallowed hard, my stomach fluttering and my throat constricting. Just knowing he still had faith in me after I'd hurt him like that was overwhelming as hell. Hearing him ask me to have that in him—and wondering how I'd ever thought I couldn't—was . . . more than I could process.

"Talk to me, Seth," he said.

"I'm not good at putting a lot of faith into anything." I touched his face and drew him closer. "But I think I can make an exception for you."

His whole body relaxed. "Thank you."

"Just so you know," I whispered, touching my forehead to his, "this scares the hell out of me."

"I know." His hand slid around the back of my neck. "Me too."

With that, he kissed me. He wasn't so aggressive this time. His kiss was almost tentative. Bordering on delicate. Maybe he wanted to savor it, maybe he was afraid even the slightest push would break this spell. He wasn't so aggressive, and neither was I, but that didn't make the long kiss any less arousing.

When we finally came up for air, we were both breathless.

I combed my fingers through his hair. "So how opposed are you to getting carried away like we did the first night?"

Darren's lips curved against mine. "Not opposed at all."

"Good."

CHAPTER 14

I couldn't say for certain how we made it from the living room into my bedroom. There was kissing—that intense kissing I'd only ever experienced with Darren—and stumbling and touching, and somehow, at the end of that, there was a bed, and then we were on that bed.

We got as far as taking off our shoes and Darren's jacket, but didn't bother with anything else. Still fully dressed, we just tangled up in each other and made out. His body heat radiated through our clothes and onto my skin. He was on top, which left my hands free, and I couldn't stop touching his face. Combing my fingers through his hair, sliding my hand across the soft beard on his sharp jaw, just touching him and memorizing his features like I hadn't felt them in years. I couldn't begin to give a damn about getting his clothes off.

But the longer we kissed and held on to each other, the tighter our grasps became. The more handfuls of clothing got in the way. The more we slipped hands under shirts and swore at belts and zippers and thick layers of denim.

He broke the kiss. "We didn't . . . We have condoms left, don't we?"

"Plenty."

"Good."

I grinned. "Are you suggesting I should get one?"

"I don't think 'suggesting' is quite a strong enough word."

That was all I needed. The clothes came off faster than I'd thought possible. Maybe something ripped or snapped, but oh well. And as soon as we were both completely naked, I sat up to put on the condom. I was tempted to lay him out on the bed again and kiss him, but that would just keep us from what we both wanted. Fuck foreplay.

Finally, the condom was on, and so was the lube, and Darren couldn't wait any more than I could. He dragged me down on top of him. I thought I even heard him curse a few times in between breathless kisses.

I sat up, and he spread his legs for me. He took me easily, moaning and shivering as I pushed a little deeper with every stroke.

"Faster," he whispered. "Please."

"Exactly what I wanted to hear," I said, and fucked him faster. Harder.

Darren's back arched and his eyes screwed shut. God, he was gorgeous like this. Naked. Shaking. Sweat rolling down his temple.

I gritted my teeth and thrust harder. I couldn't fuck him fast enough, couldn't get deep enough inside him.

Then his eyes flew open. He licked his lips, and a second later, pushed himself up on one elbow, threw the other arm around me, and pulled me down into a kiss.

I touched my forehead to his, hot sweaty skin against hot sweaty skin, and the only thing that kept me from kissing him again was the desperate need for air. I could barely breathe, and just kept fucking him hard and fast anyway and didn't care if I passed out. Muscles burned and quivered from exertion, but they did what they were supposed to, and when Darren whispered against my lips, "Don't stop, Seth," I didn't give a damn about aches or fatigue or anything that wasn't fucking him all the way to an orgasm.

His hand slipped off my neck. He reached back to the grab the headboard, eyes closed and skin flushed, and I groaned as I gave him everything I had.

The very first shudder of his orgasm set mine off; his own semen dotted his abs as I took a few final, desperate, uneven thrusts inside him until my shaking arms almost gave out beneath me. I tried to stay up, but when Darren wrapped his arms around me, I gave up and collapsed over him. I pulled out, but didn't get up, and for a while, he just held me that way, stroking my hair while we both caught our breath.

I got up long enough to get rid of the condom, and then slipped into bed beside him again. Naturally, now that the dust had settled, nerves and apprehension quickly tried to work their way back in and kill the moment.

I propped myself up on my arm and touched his face, running my thumb along the edge of his short beard. "You're sure about this. About us."

Darren nodded. "Yeah. I am. Are you?"

"Yeah. And I'm sorry. For putting you in the same box as my family."

"I can't blame you for being scared. I'm sorry I flipped out over it."

"I think I'd have done the same thing." I brushed a few strands of dark hair out of his face. "You know this could still—"

"Any relationship can fail." He ran his hand down my forearm. "But it's good today. It'll probably still be good tomorrow." One shoulder rose slightly. "After that, we'll just see how it goes. I know you're a package deal. I knew from the beginning that if I was with you, then I was with an atheist. And I don't want to change that." He raised his eyebrows. "All I ask is you accept that what you see is what you get with me, too."

"I meant what I said." I caressed his face with the backs of my fingers. "That there's nothing I'd change about you."

"Likewise," he said, and pulled me down to kiss him.

A soft meow was our only warning before the cat launched himself onto the bed beside us, narrowly missing Darren's arm with his claws.

"Really, cat?" I said. "Right now?"

Darren laughed. "Way to ruin the moment, kitty." He reached toward Stanley, but the cat just gave him a disgusted look before leaping off the bed again. "Was it something I said?"

I shrugged. "Probably just pissed about earlier."

"Earlier?"

"Yeah. He, um, hates it when people argue. I'll have to beg his forgiveness with treats later on." I smoothed Darren's hair. "For now, though, I could go for a shower. You?"

"Yeah, me too." He lifted his head off the pillow as he reached for me, and just before he kissed me, added, "In a minute."

This wasn't how I'd envisioned my love life turning out. The last place I'd ever seen myself was in a relationship with—in a *bed* with—a Christian, never mind a minister.

But I'd been wrong. And tonight, I couldn't see myself anywhere but here.

I couldn't see myself anywhere but with Darren.

Because this was where I belonged.

Want more Tucker Springs?

Visit again with the titles listed below.

Where Nerves End
by L.A. Witt

Second Hand
by Heidi Cullinan and Marie Sexton

Dirty Laundry
by Heidi Cullinan

Never a Hero
by Marie Sexton

ALSO BY
L.A. WITT

For a full list, please visit /www.loriawitt.com

ABOUT
THE AUTHOR

L.A. Witt is an abnormal M/M romance writer currently living in the glamorous and ultra-futuristic metropolis of Omaha, Nebraska, with her husband, two cats, and a disembodied penguin brain that communicates with her telepathically. In addition to writing smut and disturbing the locals, L.A. is said to be working with the US government to perfect a genetic modification that will allow humans to survive indefinitely on Corn Pops and beef jerky. This is all a cover, though, as her primary leisure activity is hunting down her arch nemesis, erotica author Lauren Gallagher, who is also said to be lurking somewhere in Omaha. L.A. can be found at http://www.loriawitt.com as well as exchanging irreverent tweets with Aleks Voinov as @GallagherWitt.

Enjoyed this book? Visit RiptidePublishing.com to find more modern romance!

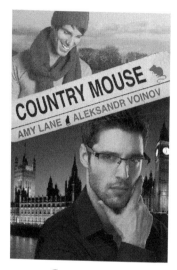

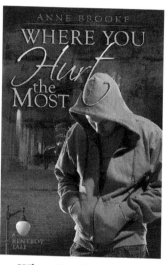

Country Mouse
ISBN: 978-1-937551-34-6

Where You Hurt the Most
ISBN: 978-1-937551-36-0

Earn Bonus Bucks!

Earn 1 Bonus Buck for each dollar you spend. Find out how at RiptidePublishing.com/news/bonus-bucks.

Win Free Ebooks for a Year!

Pre-order coming soon titles directly through our site and you'll receive one entry into a drawing to win free books for a year! Get the details at RiptidePublishing.com/contests.

Made in the USA
Charleston, SC
11 August 2013